OSLG

THE ANTIQUE LOVE

Wyoming man Kurt Bold is looking for a wife, and he's determined his choice will be based on logic. Penny Rosas is the lively and romantic owner of an antique shop in London. When Kurt hires Penny to refurbish his Victorian town house, he treats her like he would his kid sister. But it's not long before the logical heart Kurt guards so carefully is opening up to new emotions, in a most disturbing way . . .

Books by Helena Fairfax
in the Linford Romance Library:

THE SILK ROMANCE

HELENA FAIRFAX

THE ANTIQUE LOVE

Complete and Unabridged

LINFORD
Leicester

First published in Canada in 2014

First Linford Edition
published 2016

A catalogue record for this book is available
from the British Library.

ISBN 978–1–4448–2694–4

Published by
F. A. Thorpe (Publishing)
Anstey, Leicestershire

Set by Words & Graphics Ltd.
Anstey, Leicestershire
Printed and bound in Great Britain by
T. J. International Ltd., Padstow, Cornwall

This book is printed on acid-free paper

To Joe
Wish you were here

Acknowledgments

To my friend Andy, for proving
accountants can be heroes.

1

The tall man stood in the doorway for a second, his keen grey eyes sweeping the interior. There was a hush in the melodious murmur of customers, and for a couple of disorientating moments Penny's shop appeared to go into slow-mo. Then he stepped inside, his boots sounding on the wooden floor, and headed towards the display in the window. His leather satchel, slung casually from one shoulder, clinked with each footfall as he strode past Penny's counter. A few drops of rain darkened his blond head and faded shirt, and as he passed, a hint of fresh mountain air seemed to follow in his wake. Penny leaned forwards, eyes wide, following his broad shoulders as he made his way to the antiques in the window.

She touched her assistant's arm. 'See

that guy who's just walked in?' She tilted her head in the direction of the doorway and lowered her voice. 'What's the betting he's a cowboy?'

The leather boots and the hard-looking gentleman stood in the window, oblivious to the attention they were receiving. When Tehmeena failed to reply, Penny tapped her arm again and raised her voice. 'I said that guy's got to be a cowboy. What do you say?'

Tehmeena finally raised her head from her task of emptying coins into the cash till and proceeded to roll her eyes. She and Penny had been friends for a long time, and she was used to her boss's occasional flights of fancy.

'I'd say why don't you take a look outside?' she asked drily, turning her attention to her cash register. 'See any white horses tethered up?'

Penny made a pretence of swivelling her head to scan the street. She'd worked this shop floor since leaving school and knew exactly what she was going to see. Sure enough, there were crowds of exhausted shoppers crammed onto the pavement, a never-ending line of stationary cars and red buses, and drizzle. Endless grey drizzle. Yep, everything just normal for a Saturday in London. Plenty of traffic, but a distinct lack of horses.

Penny turned back to Tehmeena with a sigh. 'I guess not,' she conceded.

'We're a long, long way from the Wild West, Pen.' Tehmeena emptied the last of the bags with a short rattle of coins. 'And I don't think daydreaming is going to rustle us up a hero.'

Penny let out another sigh, this time a particularly hopeless one. Tehmeena lifted her head and regarded her thoughtfully.

'Everything all right?' She glanced over to the corner, where Penny's desk stood piled high with paperwork. 'Anything I can help with?'

'No, no.' Penny indicated the bags of coins. 'You've got enough to do. I just need to get to the bottom of all this.' She waved a hand towards the mountain of paper and smiled a little wryly. 'Sorry to leave you in the lurch.'

'No problem. And don't apologise. It's not your fault. It's all David's fault for walking out on us like this.'

Penny grimaced in acknowledgement before shifting herself from the counter to make her way to her desk. Her business partner's sudden and inexplicable storming out had certainly left them high and dry. She took her seat and picked up a pen, determined to give the accounts her utmost attention, but despite herself she found her gaze drifting back to the customer in the boots and denim shirt. The guy had to be a cowboy, whatever Tehmeena said. They might be in London, but he had the rugged outdoor looks, and he definitely had the walk. His gait was loose-limbed, as though more accustomed to striding through wide open spaces than sidestepping litter on a city street. A sense of boundless vigour clung to him, permeating Penny's cluttered antique shop. She let her wistful gaze linger a little longer before bringing her attention back to the files on her desk and choking down a sigh. Tehmeena was right, no point dreaming. The dull truth was she was in rain-soaked west London, struggling with the accounts, and just about a million miles from the mountains of Virginia.

She picked up the next file, willing herself to concentrate. A collection of invoices fell out in a heap, and the sight of David's handwritten notes amongst them only added to her depression. When the cowboy crossed her line of vision again, she lifted her head. His presence was a distraction, and it seemed it wasn't just Penny who'd noticed him. The other shoppers were straightening up in their wet raincoats, casting him surreptitious glances as he wandered around the shop. Even Tehmeena looked up from the long queue of customers, before catching Penny's eye with a grin. Oblivious to the attention he was attracting, the cowboy bent his rain-soaked head over a box of vintage postcards. Penny watched him pick his way through the pile and wondered what he would make of the long-forgotten greetings from English seasides and country cottages. Occasionally, she heard a quiet laugh break from him at some of the saucier jokes before he dropped the card back in its slot and picked up the next.

She opened up her accounts and forced herself to concentrate for a good half hour before allowing herself to look up from the papers. When she did, she was surprised to find the cowboy still there in her shop, now engrossed in the shelves of rare books. He was giving each one the same quiet attention he had devoted to everything else since he'd come in off the wet streets. She watched curiously as he reached to remove one of the editions from a high shelf, the damp fabric of his shirt tightening over his shoulders. Although the book's title was hidden in his wide-knuckled hand, Penny recognised the red binding instantly. It was a copy of Wuthering Heights, one of her favourites. As the quiet cowboy turned the pages, she tried to work out what he made of the passionate encounters taking place within. His stillness gave no clue, and his expression was hidden as he concentrated on the text. He closed the book, gave the gold lettering on the spine another close examination, and replaced it carefully where he had found it. Leaving the bookshelf behind, he moved away from Penny towards the glass cabinet containing antique china, his boots sounding the wooden floor with each step.

Penny followed his straight back before wrenching her gaze once more to her desk. The image of a starry sky and a campfire and the muted sound of guitars in the warm night flashed through her mind. She examined the next invoice. What she'd give to be away from all this paperwork and in Texas country right now. And she'd even forego the cowboy. Right now she'd settle for curling up by that campfire in solitary splendour with just a copy of Wuthering Heights for company.

She forced her tired eyes back to her paperwork.

'*FAO David Williams,*' said the invoice. '*We refer to our letter of 6th January and would remind you that we are still awaiting payment for a pair of Edwardian fluted standard lamps . . .*'

Penny tossed the invoice down with the others and shook her head. Another one. It didn't make sense. Her antique business had never had a cash flow problem. At this rate, she was in serious danger of upsetting some carefully built-up goodwill with her suppliers.

She put her head in her hands and massaged her brow. There was no sound of guitars, but at least the muted murmur of the shop's customers was quite restful.

When a booted step approached her desk, her eyes fluttered open behind her fingers.

'Excuse me, ma'am?'

The voice was low and courteous, the accent unmistakable. So, it wasn't just her imagination. Definitely a cowboy. Penny kept her hands over her face, unwilling to peep out in case the pleasant apparition disappeared. Maybe she'd fallen asleep and was dreaming. No one but a real and actual cowboy would say ma'am so politely in this part of London, unless they were talking to the Queen.

She removed her hands from her face to find her gaze on a level with a well-defined chest in a faded denim shirt. When she tilted her head, a pair of pleasant grey eyes gazed down into hers. A slow, enchanted smile banished her frown lines, and for a couple of seconds they regarded each other curiously. Close to, the cowboy seemed even truer to the stereotype. The faint lines etched around his eyes suggested a man who'd spent some time in the sun's glare, and his features had a weather-beaten ruggedness not usually found on city streets. A deep tan highlighted the lines etched on each side of a mouth which lifted slightly at the corners. She found the cowboy regarding her with the same intense scrutiny he had devoted to every other item in the shop.

Penny was suddenly conscious her face had been creased and tired when she'd looked in the mirror that morning, and that her blouse had become a little tight in recent months. She felt a little as though she were being examined and almost certainly found wanting. She lifted a hand to smooth down the hair escaping from her ponytail.

If the cowboy noticed her discomfiture, he gave nothing away, merely indicating the cash desk where poor Tehmeena was still dealing with a queue.

'I'm sorry to trouble you,' he said. 'The other lady seemed busy, so I wondered if you could help?'

'Oh, I'm sorry.' Penny pushed her chair back and stood up hurriedly. 'It's not usually like this. We're a bit short-staffed.' She ran a hand down her skirt, everything about her feeling rumpled. 'What was it in particular you were interested in?'

'I'd kinda like to look in that cabinet,' he said, indicating the antique china in the far corner. 'Would that be possible?'

Penny fumbled with a slim chain around her neck to produce a key. 'If you'd like to show me which piece?'

The cowboy gave a small nod and stepped aside to allow her to lead the way. As she passed him, she caught the scent of his rain-soaked skin and the overwhelming sensation of the great outdoors. There was a sense of grandeur about him, somehow, as though the confines of the shop were too narrow to contain him. And so as they approached the display and the cowboy indicated the vase that had caught his interest, Penny cast him a look of surprise. It wasn't a piece she would have expected a man like him to wish to see, although it was certainly unique.

'It's Victorian,' she said, raising her eyes to his curiously. 'A Coalport.'

She bent to unlock the glass door and removed the vase with care, lifting it closer so that he could see. 'It was used to hold potpourri. Made in Coalport in Wales around 1850.'

The cowboy took a step closer, bending his head over her outstretched hands and giving a low whistle. She held the tiny vase toward him a little nervously, reluctant to entrust her fragile china to such an uncompromisingly masculine figure. She was relieved to feel him take it with surprising gentleness. He placed the tiny vase with great care in one large palm, using the long fingers of his other hand to turn it this way and that.

Penny could understand his close scrutiny. The vase was a striking piece. Despite its tiny size, every available inch was ornamented with dramatic flowers in startling shades of pink and cornflower blue, deep reds and cream. Two turquoise and gold handles arched up from each side towards a lid bright with gilt. On top of the lid, the crowning glory was a handle which burst into the shape of an exuberant gold dahlia. If the cowboy was looking for quiet British understatement, then this certainly wasn't it. The vase, tiny though it was, was ablaze with ornamentation.

He ran one finger carefully over a scarlet rose. 'It's beautifully crafted,' he said in his slow way.

'Yes, it's magnificent.' There was quiet pride in Penny's voice. 'And it's typical of the style of the time. The Victorians were very fond of this type of ornament.'

The cowboy rotated the vase in his large hands, considering a reply. Penny waited expectantly.

'And they liked potpourri,' he offered eventually, his rugged features schooled into a mask of politeness.

His statement brought a quiet laugh. 'Yes, they were fond of potpourri, too,' she agreed. 'I suppose it's a bit OTT for modern taste. Nowadays we prefer things simpler. More minimalist.'

She drew nearer the cowboy and ran her own fingers over the gold dahlia.

'But I love it,' she said. Her gaze softened as she followed the curve of the flower. 'Look how every petal is detailed. It may be ornate, but there's a magnificent beauty in it.'

Her fingertips trailed further down the swell of the vase.

'And it's not just that,' she continued, eyes bright as she warmed to her theme. 'The Victorians were great lovers of romance, from their music to their literature. Look at the colours.' She gestured to the gold and turquoise handles. 'They're bursting with passion. You can almost feel the romance of it, even after a hundred and sixty years.'

Penny's exploring fingers brushed the cowboy's warm ones, and she pulled her hand away swiftly. Once again she'd found herself adrift in her own imagination. What would he think of her, burbling on like that? She lifted her head to find the warmth in his gaze had shifted a little. He dropped his eyes to the vase lying in his broad palm.

'I guess a lot of customers must fall for all that romantic stuff,' he said coolly.

She stiffened. David's last, violent outburst was still ringing round her skull. *Ridiculously romantic* was just one of the insults he'd tossed at her when he left. A dreamer. Now it seemed even this customer thought she lived in a fantasy world.

Since David's violent departure, Penny had been feeling low and out of sorts. Now the cowboy's innocent comment caught her on the raw, and to her dismay, she felt the misery she'd been fighting for days rise up and form a lump in her throat. She lowered her eyelids swiftly and reached out to take the vase. Suddenly the fingers of his free hand caught hers in a gentle grip. She raised her face to his, startled.

'I don't mean any disrespect,' he said kindly. 'I like how you describe things.

Give them their history. It kind of makes these old objects come alive.'

The warmth of his words was reflected in the quick pressure of his fingers, and Penny was touched by the generosity of the gesture. She freed her hand, bending her head to take the vase from where it rested on his broad palm.

As she busied herself replacing it in the cabinet, she wondered what on earth he must think of her, acting all stiff and English like that? And lecturing away on history. He must think she was some sort of bossy schoolmarm in her prim skirt with her hair all tied back. So it was a surprise when Penny turned round to see the stranger stretch out a friendly hand.

'My name's Kurt,' he said.

Kurt the cowboy. Of course it had to be. Penny slipped her hand into his and gave a delighted smile. 'Penny,' she said. 'Penny Rosas.'

And then he smiled back, a sudden flash of white in the rainy London afternoon.

'Penny Rosas,' he repeated. 'So that's why Penny Antiques?' He lifted his head in the direction of the window, over which the shop's name was engraved in gold lettering. 'Is this your business?'

'Yes.' With David's harsh words about her lack of business acumen still ringing in her ears, she raised her chin a little, trying not to sound too defensive. 'I started working here when I left school. Then I took over from my granddad when he retired a couple of years ago.'

The cowboy nodded slowly. 'This is a great place. Real interesting.' He let his gaze travel round the shelves of mechanical toys, the collections of fans and trinkets, and the eclectic selection of antiques, before bringing his attention back to Penny. 'I was hoping you could tell me some more. Maybe the history of some of the other items.' When Penny failed to answer straight-away, he added hopefully, 'That is, if you have time?'

Penny thought of the accounts, desperate for her attention. She hesitated, torn between putting the customer first — not too hard to do with this ruggedly charming cowboy, if she were honest — and giving a polite excuse. Kurt pre-empted her, smiling again in a way that even a saint would have found hard to resist.

'I was particularly interested in the jewellery.' He indicated the collection of antique gold and silver locked in a case near the window. 'I need to buy a present for someone.'

That clinched it. Although Penny was knowledgeable about antiques of all kinds, jewellery was her passion. She smiled widely. 'My assistant says when I get onto my jewellery I talk too much, so stop me when I get boring.'

Kurt showed no sign at all of boredom as she displayed the pieces. He listened intently, his eyes following Penny as she gesticulated with animation. When she held up a particularly striking pendant for his inspection, the gemstones caught the light from the window, and he lifted his dark blond head with a slow smile, enjoying her enchantment. In the glow of enthusiasm, she forgot all about her weariness and her anxiety regarding the accounts.

It wasn't until they reached the final item that she faltered. She reached a hand towards the last silver chain and then recollected herself, retreating swiftly to pick up one of the gold pendants they had already examined. Her movements lost their fluid grace all of a sudden and became strangely stilted.

Kurt remained where he was, gazing at the last pendant. When he turned to Penny, she thought she saw flash of understanding in him that was at odds with his apparent slowness of movement. She almost reached out a hand to tug him away, but realised any attempt to move this solid male would be futile. Her heart sank as he tilted his head in the direction of the pendant she was willing him to ignore.

'What about this one?' He slid his hand gently under the gemstones and tilted them up to the window. A cluster of tiny rose diamonds caught the light, and the pendant sparkled against his tanned hand. He lifted it a little higher, allowing the delicate chain to spill over his broad fingers.

'Now this is real beautiful,' he said slowly.

If he'd noticed Penny's reluctance, he was wilfully ignoring it. He tilted his head and waited patiently for her to speak.

'It's Art Nouveau,' she said at last. 'Turn of the century.'

The stones of the pendant gleamed softly against Kurt's hand. 'May I take a closer look?'

She gave a reluctant nod, all spontaneity completely flown. She observed Kurt's careful handling of the pendant with tight constraint. He lifted the chain from its brass hook and let it slip lightly through his fingers until the gemstones came to rest in his open palm. A single strand of silver curled neatly into the shape of a heart, from the base of which trembled several tiny rose diamonds. At the apex of the heart, two further silver strands twined around each other and then parted, one strand curving into a delicate petal, the other dropping downwards to hold two pale pink, lustrous pearls right in the heart's centre. The pearls shimmered in Kurt's hand, bringing with them all the secrets of the ocean from which they'd been plucked more than a hundred years before. It was magical.

Penny studied Kurt's expression and bit her lip. Of all the pieces in the shop, of course this had to be the one he admired the most.

'It's a love token,' she told him. Then she shook herself. 'Well, that's obvious. I mean, it's a heart . . . '

She let the sentence trail away. Kurt didn't need any of her pathetic words to describe the wonderful gems shining in his hand. In any case, after his dismissive remarks about using romance to sell to customers, she wasn't sure she wanted to continue. The gems positively glowed with romance. It was her favourite item in the whole shop, and she couldn't bear to hear his cynicism.

He moved a slow, careful finger over the pearls in the centre of his palm, and she was suddenly afraid that the pendant she loved so fervently was literally in the wrong hands. There was something in the way Kurt was studying it — something a little too remote, too controlled. All the warmth and charm in those grey eyes didn't mask the reserve in the way he carried himself and the distance he kept from people.

Penny knew she was being *ridiculously romantic* again, but she didn't care. Kurt didn't seem remotely like a guy who'd ever known what it was to love. It would be a tragedy to see her delicate love token around the neck of a casual fling, a girl the cowboy was dating just to while away his time in London. The pearls and the silver heart enclosing them were things of rare beauty, with a life all of their own. There was no way she was going to let them go to a man as unemotional as this one appeared to be. They deserved more.

But she didn't want to judge Kurt before giving him a chance. There was nothing for it but to ask him a personal question and hope he didn't think she was crazy. She cleared her throat.

'The person you're buying for,' she said. 'Is she a close friend?'

Kurt looked up from the pendant, meeting her gaze with quick understanding. He gave a brief laugh. 'Do you mean am I buying for a girlfriend?' He shook his head. 'No.'

He seemed to find the thought amusing. Penny released her breath in relief as he replaced the pendant on its tiny brass hook.

'I'm looking for a present for my sister,' he continued.

'Oh.' So it wasn't a girlfriend. Penny gave him a brilliant smile out of all proportion to his answer and then quickly tried to wipe it off her face in case he thought she was some sort of idiot. Her beloved pendant was back in its cabinet, safe from the hands of this reserved customer, and at that moment, that was all she cared about.

'In that case, perhaps a love token wouldn't be quite appropriate.'

Kurt laughed again. 'I don't think so,' he said. 'My sister would tell me I've finally lost my mind.'

'Oh,' Penny said again. She tried to imagine the taciturn man joking with his sister. Maybe he wasn't as guarded with the people close to him as he appeared. For the past half hour in her company, he'd barely spoken. He'd just kept his watchful eyes on her whilst she did all the talking.

'You seem very attached to that heart,' he said now. 'I'd say you didn't even want to sell it.'

'Oh, I'd love to sell it,' Penny cried,

then stopped short before her stupid tongue ran away with her again. The intense emotional attachment she sometimes formed for the shop's items had been one of the things about her that often annoyed David. Part of what he meant when he'd dubbed her *ridiculously romantic*, she supposed. She considered making up some reason for not selling it to Kurt — maybe tell him something about it being half-promised to another customer — and then suddenly it seemed important to her that this quiet stranger understood.

'It's not that I don't want to sell it,' she said, trying to choose her words. 'It's just that it has to go to the right person.' She wrinkled her forehead whilst Kurt waited. He seemed to guess how important this was to her. In the end she lifted the end of the pendant with one swift finger. The stones danced and shimmered back to life.

'Just look at it,' she said. Didn't he see? 'I could fall in love with the beauty of it. Think of the hours of work and the craftsmanship and the century of history behind it. The person who leaves the shop with this pendant will buy it because he has to have it. And he won't be buying it on a whim. He'll be buying it for the woman he loves with a passion.' She stepped back, cheeks heating, aware she'd finished her declaration on what was an eccentrically dramatic note. She lifted her chin, expecting mockery, and was surprised to discover a kind of warm appreciation in Kurt's gaze.

'Passionately in love,' he repeated. His downturned smile, rather than mocking Penny, appeared to be directed at himself. 'I guess that's why you didn't want to show it to me, huh?'

Penny's face heated even more as she looked up at him, but he merely shrugged good-naturedly. 'You got me weighed up all right. Those pearls should go to a better man.'

Penny kicked herself. Once again she

had let her imagination run away with her, and it would have served her right if Kurt took offence. It was fortunate for her he appeared to take her words with good humour. He moved away and held up one of the sets of earrings she'd shown him previously.

'These are perfect,' he said. 'My sister will love them.'

Penny agreed. The earrings he'd picked out — droplets of sapphire and sparkling Austrian crystal — were the perfect choice for a sister. A few minutes later Penny took Tehmeena's place behind the till and wrapped the earrings into a neat parcel, so Kurt could send them to the States.

When the transaction was concluded, she found herself reluctant to say goodbye to her cowboy. She guessed he was in London on a sight-seeing trip. It was one of those curious twists of fate that brought him into her shop, where his world and hers had so briefly touched. He would soon be leaving the congested city and returning to the freedom of his ranch, she supposed. It was with real regret she reached out her hand in farewell over the counter.

'Well, goodbye,' she said. 'It's been nice to meet you. I hope you enjoy the rest of your stay in London.'

Kurt took her hand in his and held it for a moment, smiling down at her.

'My stay here is going to be a long one,' he said. 'And as a matter of fact, I think you can help me. I need to furnish a new house, and your sign outside says you do interior design.' He pointed to a poster Tehmeena had displayed in the shop window.

'Well, it's not interior design exactly,' she said in surprise. 'It's more sourcing objects for interiors. Antique furnishings, artwork, and such like.'

'Perfect,' he said. 'That's just the sort of help I need.'

'So you're staying in London for a while?' Penny hoped the smile on her face hadn't turned into an idiotic grin.

He nodded, and her smile widened even further.

'That's great,' she said. 'Although actually, it's Tehmeena who looks after that side of the business.' She gestured to where Tehmeena stood deep in conversation with one of their regular customers. 'She's tied up at the minute, but I'll get you her card.'

She was reaching into a drawer under the counter when the slow voice spoke again.

'It's not your assistant I want,' he said. 'It's you.'

Penny lifted her head. He was regarding her with an unnerving direct-ness, as though he'd just said the most natural thing in the world. She scanned his face, trying without success to read what she saw there.

'Tehmeena has a good eye,' she said carefully. 'And a lot of experience. I'm sure she'll be able to help you.'

Kurt glanced over to the bookshelf where Tehmeena was still engaged in lively discussion.

'She seems very efficient,' he agreed. 'But I doubt she has what you have.'

'Really?' Penny said. 'And what's that?' There was a note of caution in her voice. To her mind, rare qualities didn't necessarily mean good. David had made that quite clear when he left, and she wasn't sure she wanted to hear more.

'You've got passion,' Kurt said simply.

His unexpected reply robbed Penny of speech. She checked his features for any hint of irony, but his gaze was direct, and the set of his chin suggested nothing other than plain speaking. Penny, recently dumped business partner and disappointing daughter of glamorous parents, had passion. No one had ever said anything like that to her in her life. She was literally dumbstruck.

The cowboy, mistaking her silence, proceeded to elaborate. 'You have a love for your antiques and a way of describing them that makes them come alive, like the people who owned them just walked out the door. You've got a rare gift of feeling. Hell, you love your antiques more than making a sale.' His eyes twinkled, and Penny remembered her reluctance to sell him the love token. She opened her mouth to begin an apology, but Kurt held up one hand with a shake of his head. 'You're unique, believe me, and that's why I'd love to get your help.'

It was the longest speech Kurt had made. Penny drew in a deep, astonished breath. 'Well, in that case, the least I can do is listen.' She gestured to the corner, where her desk overflowed with paperwork. 'Would you like to take a seat?'

2

It was a while before Penny managed to shuffle her papers into enough order to create space on her desk. Her tiny corner of the shop could hardly be called an office; it just happened to be the only available place to do the paperwork. After the way she'd spoken to this customer and now the unprofessional state of her desk, Penny couldn't for the life of her imagine why he was so insistent on dealing with her alone.

When she finally settled down and put everything to rights, she was bursting with curiosity. Kurt was regarding her attempts to tidy with unruffled patience, the picture of a man who was never hurried. It was a little unnerving.

Penny pressed her fingertips together and tried to sound cooler than she felt. 'So, you've just bought a flat?'

'Well, it's not exactly what you would call a flat.' Kurt lifted the leather flap on the satchel he was carrying and drew out some papers. 'This is it.'

He pushed a folder across the desk towards her. Penny noted the name of one of London's premier estate agents embossed on the cover. When she turned the page, her jaw dropped, and she had to suppress a low whistle. Property prices in London were astronomical. Even a one-bedroom flat, or apartment as Kurt would call it, was expensive to buy, but the property he was showing her was no poky bedsit. The exterior photo showed what must be at least a five-bedroom detached house, and besides that it appeared to look straight out onto Richmond Park, one of the most expensive areas in London. By London standards, it was a magnificent mansion.

The romantic picture Penny had formed of Kurt shifted. Did wandering cowboys really sell up and have enough money to buy detached houses in Richmond-on-Thames? Otherwise, where on earth did he get the cash? Had he robbed a bank? He certainly looked capable of it.

'I know what you're thinking,' he said.

'You do?' Penny looked up, unnerved. She'd actually been thinking Kurt looked just the type of character who would rob banks with great charm. A sort of modern-day Butch Cassidy. Luckily for her Kurt's mind seemed to run on rather more prosaic lines than her own.

'You're thinking this house is too large for one guy. But the fact is, I'm getting married.'

'O-o-h.' Now all became clear. Of course a guy like this had to have a girlfriend somewhere. And surely Penny wasn't stupid enough to feel disappointed? Her quick imagination threw up a picture of Kurt's likely fiancée. Tall, willowy, brilliant green eyes and flame-red hair. The sort of resourceful girl who knew how to throw a lasso and build up a campfire. Definitely not a short, plump and overworked shop-worker.

'Now I understand,' she said on a long breath. 'But surely your fiancée would want to choose the furnishings herself?'

'Well, it's kinda complicated. I don't have a fiancée yet, as such.'

'Oh?' Penny said. Her mind ticked over again and leapt to what for her was the most romantic conclusion. 'I see. You mean you haven't asked her to marry you yet?'

'No, not exactly. I mean I haven't decided on a girlfriend just yet.' Kurt was absolutely deadpan. He carried on steadily. 'I've got one or two women in mind, but I'm not in any hurry.'

Penny stared at him, wide-eyed.

'So let me get this straight,' she said. 'You want me to help you furnish a house, so you can bring a wife back to it? And you haven't decided which of your dates you're marrying?'

'Yes.' He paused. 'Is it a problem?'

'No, no.' Penny dropped her gaze and

35

fiddled with the pen on her desk. 'It's just ... well, isn't it ... I mean, everything about it,' she finally blurted out. Kurt watched in surprise as the pen clattered across the desk. 'I suppose this isn't my business — ' she continued. Kurt opened his mouth to speak, but Penny carried on, swept away by her own momentum. 'I mean you wanted me to help you with the passion thing and everything, so perhaps I should give you a hint. Women prefer it if you're actually in love with them before you propose. And they're certainly not happy about being one of a number of options.'

'I understand.' Kurt's lips twitched, but underneath the humour Penny could sense he was deadly earnest. 'And don't get me wrong, I take getting married very seriously. But I'm looking for a marriage based on mutual respect and shared interests. When I decide to get married, I want it to be a rational decision. Passion is a fickle thing.'

Penny stared at him. It was on the tip

of her tongue to say that, surely, romantic love and mutual respect weren't incompatible. She'd known long-lasting marriages based on passion — her own grandparents' for example — but something in the cowboy's manner made her feel as though she'd come up against a solid wall. The topic was obviously closed. She deliberated silently for a couple of minutes, looking into his cool grey eyes. Eventually she shut his folder and pushed it back across the desk.

'This is a much bigger project than I'd expected,' she said. 'I'm sorry, but I really don't think I'll be able to find the time.'

If Kurt was disappointed, he gave no sign of it. He merely tilted his head, his amiable gaze on hers. He seemed in no hurry to retrieve the folder — seemed to have all the time in the world, in fact. Penny had the sudden notion that despite his outwardly easy-going appearance he was the sort of man who would wait as long as it took to have things the way he wanted them.

For a couple of seconds, neither of them spoke. The folder lay in a kind of no-man's-land on the desk between them. It was like a sort of cowboy stand-off. Penny found herself subconsciously dropping her hands to her sides. The silence spread uncomfortably until, to her great annoyance, she was the first to crack.

'We're absolutely swamped with work at the moment.'

Kurt glanced at the folder and raised his eyes to hers without comment. She knew her excuse must sound lame. When he still didn't speak, she felt compelled to offer an explanation. 'My business partner David looked after our accounts, but he left a couple of weeks ago. I'm trying to get to grips with the finances as well as run the shop.'

She didn't elaborate. She'd already told him enough. There was no need to mention David's sudden and dramatic outburst when she'd mildly queried a missing invoice. No need, either, to mention that he'd accused her of being too full of romantic ideals to run a successful business. David would probably think she was being pathetically idealistic now, turning down business with an obviously affluent customer just because he didn't share her attitude towards romantic love. However, David wasn't here anymore, and in any case, it was her decision.

Penny raised her chin as Kurt ran his assessing gaze over the untidy desk and then over the rest of the shop. Her protest that they were overworked was evidently true. Poor Tehmeena was still dealing single-handedly with a long queue of customers.

Kurt brought his gaze back to meet hers. 'I understand how busy you are,' he conceded. 'But I'm in no hurry. You can do the house at a time to suit you, and take your time over whatever needs to be done.'

It was a generous offer. Even Penny realised that under normal circumstances it would be absurd to carry on refusing. Still, despite what David thought, she had a lot of common sense when it came to business. With the accounts in such a parlous state, sorting her finances had to be a priority. Her refusal to take on Kurt's business wasn't just a personal whim. She genuinely needed to spend some precious time sorting out the mess David had left her in.

'I'm not interested in getting too involved with this project,' Kurt continued, tapping the folder. 'I'm happy to turn it all over to someone else, but that means I need someone I can trust. You're the first person I've met in this city that fits the bill. You're passionate about your business, and you won't fob me off with a bunch of stuff I don't need. Whatever price you name, I'm willing to pay.'

Penny's eyes widened. His offer was certainly flattering, in more ways than one. And given the increasingly demanding invoices from suppliers which were landing on her desk, the money was definitely tempting.

'That's very generous of you,' she said, 'but — '

Kurt held up a hand. 'I understand,' he said. 'What am I thinking? Of course, you need to know more about me.'

He reached into the leather satchel again. For an instant, the ridiculous notion crossed Penny's mind that maybe the satchel contained a gun, and so it was with a sense of anticlimax that she watched Kurt pull out a business card. Penny forgot all her reservations and said the first thing that came into her head. 'Oh, I didn't know cowboys had business cards.'

The look of astonishment on Kurt's face turned her cheeks pink. What on earth must he think of her? Maybe David was right after all.

'I'm sorry,' she said. 'Sometimes my tongue runs away with me. I suppose we're a long way from Texas.'

'Well now, that's true,' Kurt said in his slow way. 'Texas sure is a long way from here. But just to set the record straight, I'm from Wyoming.'

'Wyoming!' Penny's eyes grew round with wonder. Of course, cowboy country. Maybe her imagination wasn't so far off the mark, after all. 'That sounds so romantic. I've always longed to go to Wyoming.'

'Is that so?' He was beginning to speak with a careful tolerance that ought to have been a hint, but Penny was oblivious.

'Oh yes,' she cried. 'Ever since I saw Brokeback Mountain.'

A deep laugh rumbled from Kurt's chest, and the corners of his eyes crinkled with amusement. 'Wyoming sure is beautiful country.'

The laughter in his eyes was so infectious it brought an answering smile to Penny's lips, and for a couple of seconds, they smiled at each other, as though sharing some secret joke.

'Have you travelled much?' he asked.

Penny's amusement fled. She dropped her gaze and shuffled some of the papers on her desk. It hadn't taken this guy long to weigh her up or to work out she had led a sheltered life.

'No,' she admitted after a pause. To soften the abruptness of her reply, she looked up, forcing a smile. 'I'm a city girl. The most I've travelled is a few trips to the seaside.'

A lifetime of hurt lay behind these simple sentences. Penny was so accustomed to concealing her history from strangers that brevity had become second nature. Kurt would have been astonished to know that the yellowing postcard in a frame on this plain shop-worker's desk had been sent to Penny by the film star Megan Rose. Although Penny's mother had been dead for many years, her beauty lived on, and her tragic early death only contributed to her lasting fame. The postcard showed a palm-fringed beach in Hawaii, and on the reverse, hidden inside the frame, was the simple inscription *To Penny, Home soon. Love and kisses, Mum and Dad xx*. It was the last communication Penny ever had from her parents, before they were drowned at sea off Hawaii's beautiful coast.

For a wild moment, Penny imagined pulling the card out and showing it to Kurt. 'I haven't travelled much myself, but my mother filmed all over the world,' she could say. 'She was Megan Rose. You may have heard of her?'

Her eyes flitted over the palm beach in the frame and then away. She knew revealing her background was just a fleeting thought. She'd grown weary of people's reaction on the rare occasions when she let slip who her mother was. Disbelief unfailingly turned to a sort of pitying surprise, which people were always too late to hide from her. She knew she was plain in comparison. She just got a little tired of being reminded of it by strangers.

'So, you were going to give me your card?' she prompted.

This time it was Penny's turn to be surprised. Kurt drew back in his chair.

His previously cool demeanour seemed to crack a little, and she could have sworn he was embarrassed. He looked down at the business card in his large hand, flicking the edge of it once or twice as though unwilling to part with it. The thin card made a loud thwacking sound in his fingers before he finally reached across the desk to place it in front of her.

Penny picked it up. The white card was neat and understated. In one corner was a dark blue logo: *WR*. The words *White River LLP* were printed in the same shade of blue, and under the logo, in black, was the name Kurt Bold. Beneath his name was his title: Managing Partner.

'White River,' Penny cried. 'Is the river really white?'

Kurt looked at her blankly.

'I mean on your ranch,' she went on. 'That's why it's called White River, right?'

'Not exactly,' he said. Again, the tiny hesitation combined with, this time, a

45

definite awkwardness lurking in his features. 'It's been a long time since anyone I work with has seen a wild river. I hate to disappoint you, but I'm not a cowboy, and I don't work on a ranch.'

'Not a cowboy!' Penny stared, trying hard not to let her astonishment show. How could this be? He came from Wyoming, and he looked like he'd walked straight in from the wide open spaces. He had that heart-stopping slow drawl and the smile. And then the clothes. Plenty of Londoners wore jeans, but they didn't all carry them off like he did. He was masculine, and he had strength and ruggedness and sheer capability. If a bull did decide to rampage round her antique china — although Penny could never for the life of her think of any circumstance where this was likely to happen — Kurt Bold looked just the type of guy you could rely on to catch it and throw it to the ground without breaking into a sweat.

'Don't you even work on a ranch?' she asked hopefully.

'No,' he said. 'I told you. I'm Managing Partner at White River.' He cleared his throat before announcing, 'I'm an accountant.'

'O-o-h.' Penny's mouth rounded again. She held his gaze, her disappointment slowly turning to understanding and then, finally, to mortification. He waited patiently whilst she computed his words, amusement mingled with the awkwardness still there in the twist of his mouth. A rather pitying amusement, it seemed to Penny.

'Oh, of course,' she said, lifting his card. 'White River. Now I remember. Of course everyone knows White River.'

She felt herself babbling. Everybody did know White River. Despite its romantic name, White River was a global finance firm with renowned environmental credentials. Their new offices had recently opened in London. In fact, they were just around the corner from her shop. Media coverage had been widespread, not least because of the building's green, plant-clad walls, its solar panels, and its spectacular rooftop garden. Even before the world financial meltdown had shamed the rest of those in power into examining their right to wealth, White River's directors were already ploughing their bonuses into charitable projects. It was a company renowned for combining global success with philanthropic actions.

If Penny hadn't had her head filled with mush, she'd have remembered straightaway. And, what was worse, if Kurt Bold was Managing Partner in White River, that meant he wasn't a cowboy, or even just an accountant, he was a serious somebody in global finance. Which meant he must think she was a total idiot.

Her cheeks burned.

'It's OK,' he said, looking at her not unkindly. 'It's a simple mistake. A lot of other folks have made it.'

'Really?'

He broke into his rich laugh. 'Well, no, if I'm honest, this is the first time. But I kinda like it.'

His warmth was so good-hearted, Penny found herself smiling back. For several minutes their gazes merged, until she registered a shift in Kurt's mood. For a fleeting moment his eyes darkened, but then he flicked a glance at the papers on her desk, and when he looked up, any emotion she thought she'd seen had vanished.

Penny shook herself and straightened up in her chair.

'Well, now we've got that misunderstanding over. I'd honestly love to help, but the fact is, sorting my accounts is going to take up most of my time. Maybe I can find you someone else.' She reached into her drawer to look for a list of suppliers.

'If it's just your accounts that are bothering you then I have a solution.' He leaned forward. 'Why don't I come in a couple Saturdays and take a look?'

'What?' Penny's mouth dropped

open. 'Well, that's very good of you, but I couldn't possibly afford — '

'On the house,' he said. 'Penny, you've given me an interesting morning, going out of your way to tell me the history of your antiques and all, and I feel I owe you. Besides that, if this is the only way to get your help, then I don't have any other option.'

He offered a defeated smile which didn't fool Penny in the slightest. It seemed to her the outwardly placid Kurt had somehow manoeuvred the conversation expertly until the matter was settled to his satisfaction. At a loss, she held out a hand, only to find him catching hold of it.

'Great, so we have a deal,' he said with a wide smile, enveloping her fingers in his. He shook her hand in a firm, easy grasp. 'I'm free on Tuesday lunchtime, would that suit you? There's a pub across the road. How about lunch there, and we can go through a few of the preliminaries?'

'Tuesday's fine,' Penny said, 'but — '

'Fantastic.' He rose from her desk and towered over her, blocking the light. 'I've loved meeting you, Penny, but I've taken up too much of your time already. Looking forward to seeing you Tuesday.'

Penny stumbled to her feet, but the slow-talking man was quicker than she anticipated and was almost at the door before she managed a faint goodbye. He swung the door shut, the shop's bell ringing in his wake, leaving Penny staring after him. Through the glass, she could make out his broad shoulders, the pale shirt moving easily through the lunchtime crowds on the street outside, until he reached the corner and disappeared from view.

She turned to find Tehmeena standing right next to her, following Kurt's exit with as much curiosity as Penny.

'So, what did your cowboy want?' she asked, agog.

'Actually he's not a cowboy, after all.' Penny picked up his business card. 'He's actually the head of White River, ridden into town to help us with our accounts. In exchange, we get to furnish his house. Oh, and he'll pay us top whack, even though I thought White River was the name of his ranch in Wyoming.'

'You didn't.' Tehmeena's eyes widened, then she began to laugh out loud, her pretty mouth open wide. 'You and your daydreaming. *White River*. That's priceless.'

A few weeks ago, Penny would have laughed along but not since David's hurtful outburst. Now it seemed even Tehmeena thought she was ditsy. Penny picked up the folder Kurt had left and flipped through it without looking up.

There was silence for a couple of minutes, and then Penny felt her friend's hand touch her shoulder.

'Hey,' Tehmeena said quietly. 'I'm not doing a David. I know he used to have a go at you all the time, but you should take no notice. You've got a brilliant imagination. And customers love you for it.'

'Mmm.' Penny returned the brochure to her desk.

Tehmeena squeezed her shoulder affectionately. 'And you've got the head of White River doing our accounts. That's one in the eye for smarmy David, anyway.' She lifted one dark eyebrow. 'You must have really impressed him.'

Penny shrugged. 'I didn't say anything.' She slipped Kurt's card into the folder with the rest of his paperwork. 'It's just that he didn't want to give up. The more I kept telling him we didn't have time to work with him, the more persistent he became. I expect he's the sort of man who likes a challenge.'

Tehmeena cocked her head. 'Well, I saw the way he was looking at you, hon.' A mischievous grin appeared. 'If Penny Rosas is the challenge, seems to me the cowboy from White River was enjoying playing the game.'

Penny looked up quickly. 'Ha ha. Very funny. Now you're the one with the imagination.'

'Uhuh.' Tehmeena refused to budge.

'Let's see how long it is before he asks you out.'

Penny stared. 'Asks me out?' she repeated. 'Kurt Bold is looking for a marriage based on logic and rational decisions. Do you really think that's me?'

Tehmeena's grin was so broad it nearly met her ears. 'You know what they say. Opposites attract.'

'Yeah, right.' Penny finally smiled back. Tehmeena looked so ridiculously hopeful, she couldn't help but laugh. 'Opposites do attract. I'll give you that. But I think you'd need a pretty big magnet for this one.'

⋆ ⋆ ⋆

Kurt clicked the green button on his screen and waited whilst his laptop dialled through to Wyoming. The tone sounded several times without response, and he was on the verge of disconnecting when his sister's face suddenly filled the screen.

'Hey Kurt. Sorry for the wait. I was just feeding Selina.'

'Girls keeping you busy, Ann?'

'Yeah, I guess,' his sister said. Her petite features were looking a little wan, despite her tan. 'Selina slept through the night last night, though, so that's helped. And Caitlin's a doll. She tries to help with the chores. And she told me today she's too big a girl to cry now that she's four.'

Kurt laughed. 'Guess four's a big age,' he said. 'Give them both a hug from their uncle. Wish I could be there to help you with those chores.'

He kept his tone light, but his concern was evident in the way he leaned forward towards the screen. Ann shook her head swiftly, the microphone catching the faint tinkling of her earrings. 'There's no need. You've already done plenty. I paid someone to clear the garden with the last money you sent. Caitlin has a swing and a slide and everything a little girl could want.'

Everything a little girl could want,

except a father. The words went unspoken between them. Ann's latest boyfriend had left her, just the same as the previous one. Kurt's sister ran into relationships with boundless optimism, expecting everything to be rosy; always sure that this time it was definitely true love. But every time, the guy was either faithless or feckless. Kurt had lost count of the number of times his sister had used his shoulder to cry on. No matter how he tried to convince her, she continued to hold blindly to the belief that true love was just around the corner.

Kurt had been protecting his half-sister ever since he was twelve years old and she was just a tiny scrap in a diaper. No matter how often his little sister messed up her life, Kurt would always be there to pick up the pieces, because deep down he understood just what she was looking for with that unshakeable romantic longing. She was trying to fill the empty hole left by their childhood. But Kurt also knew that that hole would never be filled by true love, or whatever else Ann wanted to call it, because all that was just a fairy-tale. Fine in stories, but not for real life. He wished his sister would accept that, as he had done, and be content to live her life without expectation of anything more. Things would be simpler.

She looked at him now with eyes the same cool grey as his, though unlike Kurt's, hers were filled with hope.

'Anyway, what about you?' she asked. 'What's new in London?'

'I have this to show you,' he said, holding up the estate agent's brochure. 'I finally bought a house.'

'A house! Cool. What's it like? And where?'

Kurt went through the photos one by one, explaining the history of neighbouring Richmond Park. As a piece of green space it was tiny on Wyoming's scale, but Ann thought it was charming.

'So, a big house and a park,' she said, her head on one side. 'Guess now all you need is a wife and children.'

Kurt folded the photos away. He had told Ann a few days ago that he planned to marry, and she had been so excited she'd almost reached through the screen and kissed him. She wanted to know all about the girl who'd finally captured his heart. When Kurt explained that he hadn't actually proposed to anyone yet and that he wasn't in love, his sister's happiness plummeted sharply. She'd regarded him in that sad, quizzical way she always did when he did something she couldn't understand. Now as Kurt folded the estate agent's paperwork, an image of Penny popped into his head, her mouth rounded softly in surprise when he'd told her the same thing.

'Actually, I met someone today you'd like,' he said.

'Oh?' Ann's face looked so hopeful, Kurt had to laugh.

'Not in the girlfriend way. Her name's Penny. She works in an antique shop, and she's going to help me furnish the house.'

'Is she pretty?'

Kurt rolled his eyes. He was going to tell his sister, no, Penny wasn't pretty. He was ready to explain that when he'd first seen her, he'd thought her unremarkable to the point of plainness. Her oval face, pale with weariness, had been crunched tight in concentration over her papers, and her nondescript brown hair scraped back in a ponytail. When she'd stood up to speak to him, she'd been small in her flat work shoes and slightly plump. She'd looked like she badly needed some fresh air and a long vacation.

But then he thought of the way she'd lit up when she started talking about the antiques in her shop, and how the sudden vitality transformed her weary features. Her passionate animation had transfixed him. And when she'd spoken of how little she'd travelled, her blue eyes had deepened in shade. She'd lifted her face to his with such an attractively wistful smile that he'd found himself drawn to her, wanting to keep the glow from vanishing. It was as though, for a moment, she had bewitched him. And maybe she had cast some sort of spell, because now he faced giving up several Saturday mornings to go through her accounts — not something he'd ever offered to do for anyone else.

He wondered what his sister would say if he expressed these thoughts aloud and gave a wry inward laugh. *Bewitched*. The sort of thing Penny Rosas herself would say. If he was going to be working with Penny, he would have to guard against being drawn into her fanciful way of thinking.

'Yeah, I guess you could call her kinda pretty,' he said simply. 'And she helped me pick out a great present for you.' He held a padded envelope to the webcam. 'It's a surprise.'

'Aww, Kurt, she sounds adorable.' Ann looked hopefully at him from the screen.

Kurt pictured the wife he had

envisaged: cool, sensible and pragmatic, with both high-heeled feet planted firmly in reality. Not one with iris-blue eyes that were dangerously soft and wistful and full of dreams.

He looked into Ann's expectant features. 'No,' he said emphatically. 'This one's definitely not marriage material.'

3

The rain was bouncing down in fat, dirty drops on the pavement when Penny left the shop. She put her ancient leather briefcase over her head and made a quick splash over the road to the pub opposite. A welcome blast of warmth and the delicious waft of home-cooked food met her as she pushed open the door. From the outside, the Edwardian building appeared rather drab to passers-by, but the interior was a stunning surprise. Penny had long since grown accustomed to its magnificence.

She gave a rapid glance round the gilt mirrors and the splendid cream and red tiles, looking for her denim-clad cowboy-slash-accountant. When a tall, broad-shouldered man stood up from a table in the window, looking darkly handsome in a suit and tie, she didn't immediately recognise him. Then she twigged. Of course, it was a working day, and Kurt wasn't a cowboy. He actually worked in finance. That's why he's wearing a suit, she told herself, trying to damp down the rush of butterflies that fluttered into life at the sight of him.

Penny was well known, and many of the pub regulars greeted her warmly as she threaded her way across the room. She was obliged to stop several times to field enquiries regarding her health and that of her grandfather, so that by the time she reached Kurt, she had ample time to regain her usual composure. But when he pulled out a chair for her with a wide, handsome smile, she felt the butterflies flying dangerously back into life.

'Sorry I'm late,' she babbled. 'Sudden rush of customers.'

'Yes, I know. I saw,' he said. His eyes were smiling.

Penny glanced out of the window. The rain was easing, and a few lukewarm rays of sun fell across the street, picking out the gold lettering on her shop front. She had forgotten her actions would be visible to anyone sitting across the road in the pub. It had been a full morning, most of which she'd spent engrossed with customers, explaining the background to her antiques. Or *telling her stories* as David used to call it. Now she glanced at Kurt, feeling slightly awkward to have been on display.

'You look very impressive in action,' he said simply.

Penny flushed with pleasure. She was struggling to think up a reply when he moved on, lifting the battered cardboard menu from the table. 'What would you like to eat?'

The change of subject was gratefully received, and soon they immersed themselves companionably in a discussion of the pub's traditional English fare. Penny attempted to persuade Kurt to let her pay — insisting he was her customer, after all — and found herself politely, but firmly, overruled.

As she watched him make his way towards the bar, cutting a path with easy grace through the lunchtime crowd, she couldn't help but contrast his evident warmth and openness with his coldly logical approach to his love life. The two facets of his character didn't seem to mesh together. Penny's time behind the shop counter had provided invaluable experience in dealing with people. She was also intuitive and could generally sum up strangers pretty accurately, but she had to admit that Kurt was a more complex character than the usual customers she met.

She watched him give their order to a giggling barmaid and noted how he took the girl's simpering attention in his stride. He was probably used to girls falling over themselves, she thought wryly. After all, the barmaid wasn't the only woman in the pub whose wide eyes were following him. Quite a few female heads were turning and one group in particular, a table of office-workers in the far corner, had their mouths wide open and were positively drooling.

Penny shifted her gaze from Kurt's strong back to stare out of the window. It certainly didn't seem as though the guy would have to look far to find a wife. If this random group of women were anything to go by, most of them would be falling over themselves to fit the role, no matter how distant and calculated his reasons appeared to Penny. For some reason, the thought that there would be plenty of women rushing to accept Kurt on his own logical terms made her quite cross. She reminded herself forcefully that Kurt's marriage plans were nothing to do with her. Her job was simply to fit out his house in the best possible style so he could bring home a lovely wife to match the furniture.

She opened her leather briefcase with a snap and brought out the pile of papers within, arranging them in a neat pile on the scrubbed wooden table. Then she picked up the first page — a cutting she had taken from a recent home and style magazine — and regarded it dolefully. With most customers she would have garnered a fair idea by now of what made them tick. Once you knew what made a person tick, it was a short step to knowing what style would work for them. With the ambiguous Kurt, however, she'd so far been unable to connect with how he thought. His idea of what constituted a happy home seemed so far removed from Penny's own, that once again she found herself seriously doubting her ability to complete the project. She replaced the cutting on the pile and waited for Kurt to thread his way back to their table, a hundred female eyes at his back.

After placing an orange juice brimming with ice in front of her, he gestured to her stack of papers.

'I'm impressed,' he said. 'You got all this together on such short notice?'

'Just a few ideas I was going to show you for your house.' Penny looked up with a bright smile fixed to her face then quickly dropped her gaze to the table. He was taking off his jacket, for heaven's sake. She caught a glimpse of chest muscle hardening against his shirt as he leaned forward and shuffled her leaflets together to distract herself.

'Let's have lunch first,' he said, motioning her to put the papers away. 'I saw you across the street there. You've had a busy morning.'

Penny reached for her orange juice and took a grateful sip, the iciness soothing the back of her throat. It was true; she had done a lot of talking that morning. Despite what David said to the contrary, her customers loved to listen to her talk about the antiques, and she enjoyed sharing her enthusiasm with them. She put down her glass with a satisfied sigh to find Kurt's assessing gaze on her.

'You ever get any time off?' he asked,

indicating the shop front across the street.

'I used to do.' She pulled a face. 'That was before my business partner left.'

Penny's pain must have shown on her face. Kurt leaned forward. 'So what happened? He just up and left, just like that?'

Every time Penny thought of David's violent departure, there was a terrible constriction in her throat. She took another sip of her blessedly cool juice, easing the tightness.

'We had an argument.' Her voice was calm, but her fingers were clenched a little too tightly round her glass. 'It was silly, really. I don't even know how it started. I asked David to check something in the accounts, something that didn't stack up . . . '

Her voice trailed away. It was impossible and far too humiliating to continue. To tell Kurt how David, who had become increasingly volatile in the previous weeks, suddenly exploded with rage, subjecting her to a vicious diatribe in which he accused her, amongst other terrible things, of being *ridiculously romantic* and *insanely over-imaginative*.

'Guess you'd worked together a long time.' Kurt was still, watching her steadily.

She replaced her glass on the table and rubbed her tense fingers. 'He worked for my grandfather at first. Then Granddad made him partner, and after I took over the business I inherited him. He and I never really hit it off in the past, but he brought in a lot of business. There was nothing to stop us having a good working relationship, and anyway he'd been with us for ten years without a problem.'

'He worked for you all that time, and he just left?' Kurt's eyes widened incredulously. 'Left you high and dry? Guy's a rat.'

Penny didn't know what response she'd expected from Kurt, but she found his chivalrous leap to her defence quite touching. She'd been bottling up her feelings for weeks, trying not to worry her grandfather and trying to shelter Tehmeena from the worst of the extra workload. Now Kurt's unexpected sympathy had an unfortunate effect, and she felt tears begin to prickle. She bit down on her lip, turning her head to one side.

Kurt placed his hand over hers. His kindness was almost the final straw, and she was horrified to feel she might actually start crying. Then he spoke, bringing her back from the brink.

'You're better off without that asshole.' His grip tightened.

Penny gave a watery laugh, sliding her eyes round to meet his. He met her gaze with a grin.

'If you'll pardon some Wyoming plain speaking.'

Penny grinned back. For a second, he gazed down at her, his fingers tightening on hers, and to her surprise, she found herself returning the pressure. Then the barmaid arrived with their meals, batting her massive eyelashes in

Kurt's direction, and the moment was broken. Kurt withdrew his hand to make room for their plates.

Penny pulled back, glad of the distraction the food offered. Once again Kurt's actions had thrown her. She sensed that underneath his easy-going charm, he was probably a man you could thoroughly rely on. She glanced over at him, sitting at ease in his shirt-sleeves. Broad-shouldered in real life, as well as metaphorically. The sort of man any woman would be glad to have as a husband — if it weren't for the fact that he'd probably use a spreadsheet before proposing, just to make sure he'd weighed up all the advantages and disadvantages. His outlook went against every romantic fibre of Penny's being. She had the sudden notion that accountancy was a profession which must suit him right down to the ground, offering an environment of reason, logic, and order. How different his personality was from the romantic aura he carried around him. All of a sudden, she chuckled to herself. Kurt looked up from the plate in front of him.

'I was just thinking how different the life of an accountant is from the life of a cowboy.' She giggled again. 'And how ridiculous you must have thought me when you came to my shop.'

Kurt didn't smile back. He gave her comment serious consideration before offering a slow reply. 'No, I didn't think you were ridiculous. I think you're intuitive, and you have imagination — something people say I lack. That's why I wanted your help with furnishing my house.'

Penny bent her head to her meal, feeling a little overcome. She appreciated Kurt's compliment, but she didn't believe that he lacked imagination deep down. Why else was he drawn to that Coalport vase? He must have had some sort of imaginative impulse to see the beauty behind the ostentation. And then she'd known as soon as Kurt picked up her love token that he'd recognised the magic in it just as strongly as she did. It was just that he kept his imagination under tight rein. There was something permanently controlled about the way he carried himself, and she found it a little intimidating.

'Anyway, I'm glad you're an accountant and not a cowboy,' she said suddenly, looking up. 'Handling a herd of cattle is all right, I suppose, but we need someone who's good with figures. David left the books in a terrible mess.'

'No problem,' Kurt said, returning to his steak pie. 'I'm sure it won't take me long to get to the bottom of it.'

Penny watched him begin to make unconcerned inroads on his meal and for the first time in weeks felt a small lift of her spirits. Kurt was such a solid and dependable presence, she wondered if maybe he was right, and she did have intuition. She'd imagined Kurt in the role of a hero when he first stepped into the shop, and if he turned out not to be a cowboy sort of hero, what did it matter? Her guess was right. He'd ridden into town to help her with her accounts, and that was hero enough for her. The thought brought an inward smile.

She turned her attention to the lamb stew in front of her, blowing absent-mindedly at the steam. 'So,' she said, 'I should get to know you a bit better, maybe. If I'm going to furnish your house, I mean?'

'Ask away.' Kurt waved an airy knife.

The invitation to ask anything threw Penny off guard for a moment. There was so much she was dying to know. Where to start?

'OK,' she said. 'Can I ask . . . ' She put down her knife and thought for a couple of seconds. 'You said you were getting married?' Kurt nodded without looking up. 'Then maybe I should know what sort of wife you're looking for. How do you see your future in your house in Richmond? And why do you want to get married, anyway, if you don't believe in love?'

Her words came out in such an eager rush that Kurt laughed.

'That's a lot of questions,' he said, putting down his fork and giving her his attention. 'Well, to start, I've always wanted a proper family. I've made a success out of my career, and now I need someone to share my life with. I guess a family is what I'm waiting for to make the rest of my life complete.'

'So you think something's missing in your life?'

Her question silenced him for a moment.

'Missing something,' he said after a while. 'I hadn't really thought about it, but that's a good question. Maybe I am missing my family, here in England. Maybe starting a family of my own is just the logical answer.'

There it was. Logic again. Penny frowned. There was no arguing with a logical approach, but where relationships were concerned it was nowhere near enough. She felt like physically prodding Kurt until she could get him to see what she saw.

'Have you ever been in love?' she asked in desperation.

That was the question. She was startled to see all trace of amiability leave Kurt's expression. It was as though a black cloud descended on him. He leaned back, a stony expression on his face.

'No,' he said flatly. 'Love is a deception for fools. I've seen passion bring a man to his knees and ruin him. Seen it with these two eyes.' He reached a hand up to his face in what for the laconic Kurt was an unusually dramatic gesture. 'If you allow passion to rule you, then ultimately it will destroy you.'

Penny stared. Her question had certainly prodded Kurt, but his response had been more than she bargained for. Now she knew she was right. His whole demeanour showed it, from the darkening of his eyes to the coiled reserve in his body. No matter what his protestations, or how he tried to withhold it, a deep well of passion ran within Kurt, like the seam of an oil well. Is this why he kept such a tight rein on himself? Did he feel his own passionate nature was a dangerous thing? She was struggling to compute his answer when the black cloud lifted as quickly as it had come.

His expression softened. 'Don't look so concerned,' he said. 'It was a simple question, and it should have a simple answer. No, I haven't been in love. I've joined a dating agency, and you'll find this hard to believe, but there are plenty of women out there who think the same way I do.' He spread his hands. 'I'm perfectly open about what I'm looking for in a relationship, and you might be surprised to hear I've had a lot of responses to my profile.'

He looked as though he was astonished at the response himself, and Penny had to bite back a smile. She wasn't the slightest bit surprised he'd had a lot of female interest. Kurt was strong-minded, courteous, considerate, and a successful financier. He came across as real hero material. The only surprise was that the internet hadn't crashed across Europe as soon as his profile went online.

'Fine, maybe I'm asking the wrong sort of questions,' she said. 'Maybe something more about what style of house you like.' She wrinkled her brow. 'Something about your personal taste. Or I know: which artists have you been to see in London?'

For the rest of the meal, they kept the topics light. Although Penny had realised a while ago that Kurt's simple exterior was deceiving, she was surprised at his wide-ranging knowledge. He talked in a thoughtful, interested way about the shows and exhibitions he'd viewed during his time in London. She found they had a lot of shared interests, and even discovered that on one occasion, they must have been in the same art gallery at the same time without realising it.

When a companionable pause fell in the conversation, Penny leaned back in her chair. They'd been talking for quite a while, but it was one of those conversations where neither person revealed much personal information. There'd been a moment — a small opening in the conversation — when she could have told Kurt about her own background. Kurt had asked about her family, and all sorts of responses flashed through her mind. As usual, though, she'd decided to gloss over her mother's identity and merely informed him her parents had died tragically young, without elaborating.

Her gaze lit on the gilded mirrors along the wall behind Kurt, and she saw her troubled features repeated over and over as her reflection disappeared into the distance. Her frown deepened. Penny was open-hearted by nature, but past experience had taught her to be cautious. She'd been on the receiving end of a range of unpleasant reactions on the rare occasions when she'd let fall her mother was Megan Rose. Some thought she was a name-dropper, some were jealous, some thought she was trying to use her mother's name to build up her business. Some people even believed she was making it up, and that it was all just another sign of her over-active imagination. Still, she knew instinctively that none of these reactions would fit Kurt.

She brought her gaze back from the mirror. Kurt was quite still, lost in thought, his eyes on some point outside the window behind her. She examined his sturdy profile and knew straight-away it would be impossible to tell him the truth. She couldn't bear for that instant look of incredulity to cross his face, that reaction which was always closely followed by embarrassed pity. Penny had no film star looks, and she knew it. All she wanted was to be treated as a person in her own right. And she knew as soon as she said her mother's name, she would lose all confidence in herself. Penny Rosas would be second-best to her mother's memory once again.

She let out an involuntary sigh, and Kurt turned immediately, the light from the window trailing dusty gold over his blond head.

'Everything OK?' He bent towards her. 'Guess you should be heading back to the shop.'

He regarded her silently for a moment, and the dusty ray of sunlight caught them both in the same wide shaft. He gave a slow, warm smile.

'I've enjoyed our lunch,' he said, breaking the pause. 'I knew I'd gotten the right person when I chose you. Here's to working together.'

Penny raised the remains of her orange juice. 'Here's to your happy home.'

She smiled, and her glass sparkled in the pale sunlight from the window.

⋆ ⋆ ⋆

Daniel Rosas was in the kitchen making a start on the evening meal when his granddaughter arrived home after work, rain-soaked and weary.

'Hello, love, you're early.' As usual, he brightened at the sight of her. 'Is everything all right?'

'Yes, fine, Granddad.' She pulled off her wet coat. 'I don't need to work so late now, you know. Kurt's going to help me with the accounts.'

'Oh yes, the cowboy.'

The cowboy from White River story had made Penny's grandfather laugh out loud. Penny always tried to bring home a few light-hearted stories from her day to share with him over their evening meal, and he'd particularly enjoyed hearing about her meeting with Kurt. There was a time when she would have told her granddad everything — all her worries regarding the accounts and David's aggressive behaviour before he dramatically quit — but these days she kept her problems to herself. Daniel was becoming increasingly frail. Penny had noticed the change in him and could date it from the day of her grandmother's funeral two years ago. Since then, he had visibly shrunk. It was as though everything were an effort, and Penny was frightened to burden him with her worries in case he became physically ill.

Kurt's arrival was a blessing in more ways than one, since she no longer had to fret that her grandfather would discover the wretched state of the shop's accounts. Penny knew instinctively that Kurt could be relied on to sort through the shop's books with efficiency and tact.

'I'm going to see Kurt's house in Richmond at the weekend,' she told him, hoping to interest him in the project. 'I brought home some brochures and stuff.' She lifted the paperwork out of her briefcase and set it on the kitchen table. 'Thought you might be interested in helping me with some ideas.'

It was the sort of project her granddad would normally pounce on with enthusiasm. Although too fragile for the everyday stresses and strains of business, he still shared the same passion for the world of antiques as Penny. So she was dismayed when he cast an absent glance at the documents before turning away.

'OK, love, I'll have a look later.'

His hands shook slightly as he lifted a saucepan onto the cooker. When Penny stepped towards him, she noticed his lined face was paler than usual.

'Are you OK, Granddad?'

He lit a match to the ring and then shook the flame out unsteadily. 'David came round to see me this afternoon.'

'David! What did he want?'

'Said he wanted to give his side of the story. Tell me why he felt he had to leave. When I said you were in charge of the business now, that it was nothing to do with me, he started to get a little belligerent.'

'He has no right bothering you at home.' Penny strode over to the sink to pour herself a glass of water. 'He knows how things are, with Grandma dying and everything. After everything you've been through, he should be leaving you in peace to enjoy your retirement.'

The water streamed out of the tap in a furious burst.

'Yes. I know I'm officially retired, but I'm always here if you need help, Penny,' her grandfather reminded her. 'I'm not senile yet.'

She turned round to see him leaning against the kitchen units. Suddenly he seemed incredibly fragile.

'I know, Granddad,' she said. 'And I appreciate your help. That's why I brought you the paperwork for Kurt's house to look at. But as far as the accounts go, David needn't worry. Kurt's looking into them now.'

'That's what I told David,' he said. His eyes screwed up, and he rushed to finish his sentence. 'And that's when he started losing it. He started saying some terrible things. Said you were a dreamer and a romantic, and you wouldn't last two minutes in business without him. The chap's a total dope. You're well rid of him.'

Her grandfather caught hold of a chair back and gripped it. Penny hurried to place her hand over his thin one, feeling the skin pathetically taut over his bones.

'Granddad, don't worry about me. I can look after myself. And I told you, I've got help anyway. Tehmeena's great, and I've got the head of White River looking at my accounts. I'm doing perfectly well by myself. I don't need David.'

Daniel turned to the stove to stir a pan that didn't need stirring, his hand thin and shaky on the wooden spoon.

'I don't doubt you can run that business perfectly well,' he said, more quietly now. He carried on stirring, his slumped back turned towards her. 'It's not that that bothers me. You're a beautiful person, Penny,' he continued, holding up the spoon to halt her when she would have protested. 'I know you don't think so, and maybe your grandmother and I are to blame for that. You're not beautiful in the same

87

way your mother was. And your mother wasn't a romantic like you. She looked like a vulnerable heroine in all those films, but she could be extremely hard-headed. She was determined to do what she wanted and blow the consequences.'

He turned round to face her. Penny was staring at him, wide-eyed. Her grandmother had never spoken of her mother in this way. She always made her mother out to be some sort of beautiful, tragic paragon, someone who Penny could never possibly live up to.

'You're nothing like your mother but not in the way you think. You have a much warmer heart. And I worry that one day someone is going to break it.' Daniel's voice broke a little at the end of his speech, and he would have turned away then, but Penny caught hold of his hand and pulled him into a fierce hug.

'Oh, Granddad,' she said into his old sweater.

'I know you grew up in your mum's

shadow, Penny,' he said over the top of her head. 'But you're a special person.' He pulled away and looked down into her troubled face. 'So don't let anyone ever make you feel second-best. Not David, not anyone. You're worth far more than you think you are.'

Penny stilled for a moment in his embrace, touched by his words. Her grandfather's extraordinary kindness had helped keep her on an even keel after her parents' death, but still, it was hard not to feel as though her mother's legacy was permanently colouring her life. She thought about how she had concealed her identity from Kurt and felt a miserable chill run through her. She knew she should show more courage, but it was difficult living up to a woman who had been fêted as one of the iconic British beauties of the century. Once Kurt met that ideal woman of his, he would be moving out of her life, and in the meantime, as cowardly as she knew it was, it was easier not to say anything.

'It's OK, Granddad.' She turned back to the table, hiding the pain in her expression and keeping her tone light. 'You don't have to worry about anyone breaking this old heart. It's too tough now for all that.'

She began laying the table mechanically. If she'd turned round then, she would have seen that her words had failed to reassure her grandfather in the way she intended. If anything, he looked more distressed. He opened his mouth to speak and then closed it again, turning to the stove to begin serving out their meal.

4

The following weekend found Penny in the bathroom in Kurt's house, staring at the bidet, hands covering her face. She peered in dismay over the tips of her fingers. For a couple of seconds, neither of them spoke. Kurt took a step nearer, gazing down into the hideously patterned bowl.

'So, what period would you say?' His voice was deadpan, but when he raised his eyes, they were dancing at the sight of her pained expression.

She lifted her head to scan the bathroom. The hideous pattern was repeated over and over again in the tiles, from floor to ceiling.

'Late eighties,' she said at last, with a stunned shake of the head. 'Late eighties gone horribly, horribly wrong.' The colour was salmon pink, the pattern was tiny and floral and everywhere. The result was suffocating. 'I'm glad I came to see all this for myself,' she continued. 'I didn't get the full effect in the estate agent's brochure.'

'No,' Kurt agreed with a laugh. 'Estate agents don't usually state the full effect.'

He led the way out of the master bathroom and onto the landing. Here the beautiful floorboards were still intact, but the original oak grain was suffocated by too dark a shade of varnish. The space should have been magnificently light and airy since an enormous arched window lit up the stairwell, but the walls were painted a depressing combination of hunter green and cream.

Penny made her way with care down the first uncarpeted stairs to a bend in the staircase and stopped to gaze out of the window. Below was a large, rather untidy garden, bordered by a stone wall. Beyond the wall lay all the glory of Richmond Park. A faint mist rose from the park's grasslands, and a pale yellow sun was attempting to dispel the damp. In the distance was a huddle of deer, their antlers waving regally. It was a bucolic country scene. Hard to believe they were only a few miles from the City.

'I don't think anyone could ever tire of this view,' Kurt said. He had moved behind her, and when Penny turned her head, she found her eyes more or less level with his chin. His gaze was fixed on the scene below. Trapped as she was between Kurt's broad chest and the window, there was nowhere for Penny to retreat. She turned her head to examine the view outside, trying to ignore the warmth of his body at her back and pressing herself closer to the glass.

It had been mostly easy that morning to avoid getting too close. There was plenty of room in the empty, cavernous house for Penny to take a few steps away whenever she needed. But although it was easy to put physical space between them, no matter where Kurt was in the house, Penny had been aware of him. He said very little, his movements slow and self-contained, and yet he possessed a solid presence which filled the very air around her. Alone in the empty house, Penny was finally forced to recognise the strength of her physical response to him.

She concentrated on the scene below, watching the mist weave and settle over the beech trees. She had thought Kurt, too, was lost in the view, but when she stirred beside him, lifting a hand to rest against the window-frame, he surprised her by responding instantly.

'Guess you must be tired.' He touched her shoulder. 'Seems like you've written a whole novel this morning.'

Kurt had found Penny's copious note-taking amusing as she darted round the house. He told her she was like a little bird, eager to see everything. Now she lifted her face to his with a smile.

'I've got loads of ideas running through my head. But it's been fun. I've loved it.'

'Yeah, it's been fun.'

★ ★ ★

Kurt looked down into Penny's smiling face, surprised at just how much fun it had actually been. He hadn't been looking forward to the drudgery of having to fit out the interior of his new house, but since spending the morning in Penny's company, he'd found just how enjoyable a renovation of this kind could be.

In every room, there had been something for Penny to enthuse about. She drew his attention to little details he never would have noticed, making the empty, echoing place come alive. Her descriptions were so vivid, he could swear in Penny's mind the former Victorian owners were almost real.

When they first arrived in front of the arched stone doorway, she mentioned it was part of an architectural style called Gothic Revival. As proof she grabbed hold of his hand and pulled him round to the side of the building to show him a gargoyle he'd never noticed, half-hidden as it was by wisteria. She even enthused later about a filthy old oven she'd discovered in the cellar, telling him it was a quality cast iron Edwardian range which, with time and attention, could be restored to its previous glory. He'd teased her by telling her he thought it was ready for the trash, but she was outraged.

Penny brought a freshness to every dusty nook and cranny, but more than that, she had a magical way of telling a story. He could have listened to her for hours as she conjured up the sort of people who would have lived in the house. She made them seem so real, it was as though they'd just walked out the door.

Kurt took in her fresh, glowing features and was filled with a sudden warmth, an urge to reach for her that took him by surprise. He lifted a hand to touch her temple, making light of his sudden swell of tenderness.

'There's a cobweb.' He brushed the trail away. And then, because he didn't want the morning with her to end yet, he surprised himself further by adding, 'I'm going to take a walk out there in the park. Want to come with me?'

Penny flinched a little at the touch of his fingers. She stepped back, so her shoulders were pressed against the glass.

'Yuck, spiders,' she said after a minute, brushing at her fringe, her face hidden beneath the sweep of her long hair. 'You're right. Let's take a walk and get out of all this dust.'

★ ★ ★

Penny took a deep breath as soon as she stepped outdoors. A walk in the fresh air would do her good in more ways than one. The huge old house was beginning to feel too small to contain them both, and she felt again the urgency of putting as much space as possible between herself and Kurt.

Noon was chill and misty when they reached the park. Although a scattering of hopeful crocuses had pushed their way through the grassland, the chill damp of winter continued to hang in the air. She had swathed herself in a woolly scarf and hat. Only her eyes and broad cheekbones were showing, invigorated by the fresh air. Kurt had thrown on a thin fleece. She could see him visibly relaxing as they left the traffic-filled streets and entered the wide green space of the park.

'Aren't you cold?' She knew the answer to the question before she'd even asked it. Kurt seemed to radiate health and vitality, even more so now they had reached the outdoors. He looked at her across the couple of feet of distance she had made between them and laughed, his outbreath joining the mist.

'This isn't so cold. You should see the ice and the snow in Wyoming. Now that's cold.'

'Do you miss it?' she asked curiously, lifting her head from the path they were treading. 'Home, I mean?'

'I miss the scale of it all. The sky and the mountains. I don't like to feel too boxed in.'

They trod the muddy path in silence for a while. Penny wondered what it must be like to be living abroad, far from family and in an alien landscape. She couldn't imagine leaving her grandfather and her shop and being happy. Kurt spoke again, almost as though he'd read her thoughts.

'I miss the landscape, but I wouldn't call Wyoming home. Apart from my sister, there's no one there I miss.'

It was the first time since they met that Kurt had revealed anything of himself unprompted. He was looking straight ahead, apparently concentrating on the scene unfolding as they moved through the thin mist.

'Don't you have anyone else? Other family?'

He gave a small shake of the head. 'Like you, my mom died when I was small. My dad died a couple years back. My sister's really my half-sister. And my step-mom's around somewhere, but me and my sister, we haven't heard from her for years.'

For someone as taciturn as Kurt, it was a long and revealing speech. Penny bent her attention to the path for a while, the moisture from her breath fading and falling. The leaves from the previous autumn were sodden and decaying underfoot, masking the sound of her boots. When she drew in a deep breath to speak, the sound was clear in the cold air.

'Haven't you ever tried?' she asked. 'To contact your step-mum, I mean?'

Kurt kept up his loose-limbed stride, both hands in the pockets of his fleece. When he didn't answer immediately, she carried on impulsively. 'I mean, family's important, isn't it? Doesn't your sister miss her mum?'

This finally made Kurt stop on the footpath and turn to her. 'You ever see Snow White?'

Penny barely had time to nod before he turned back to the path and started walking again, leaving her to catch up.

'Well, when I was a kid, I used to think they must have based that movie on my step-mom. I thought my dad's new wife was the evil stepmother come to life. Dad worshipped the ground she walked on. She was pretty, and she was twenty years younger than him. No matter how she treated me and Ann, he just didn't see it. She was cruel and selfish, but he loved her blindly, with a passion.'

They passed under a leafless tree, the branches just starting to bud. Kurt reached out to snap off one of the dead twigs and began swishing it as he walked, the thin wood making a hissing sound in the still air.

'I was twelve, and Ann was just a baby when my step-mom left us all for some guy she met in a bar. Some guy richer than my dad. But that didn't stop her taking pretty much all the cash from Dad's hotel business with her when she left. Left us all high and dry.' He cast the twig aside. 'Dad was a broken man after that.'

In the silence that followed, they heard the muffled sound of hooves in the mist. Kurt slowed to a halt, lifting his head before turning to face Penny. There was no bitterness in his features, just a sort of weary resignation.

'So you see that passion and love stuff isn't all it's cracked up to be. It broke us as a family. My sister didn't have a great childhood after that.'

'Neither did you,' Penny cried. She was beginning to realise how like Kurt's chivalry it was to think only of his sister and not himself. And how all of this made a lot of other things about him fall into place, too. Seeing the look on her face, Kurt smiled, lifting a gentle finger to touch what could be seen of her cheek between her hat and scarf.

'Guess that makes three of us,' he said. 'You remind me a little of my kid sister.'

The sound of horses' hooves was nearing, and Kurt swivelled round, missing the wince that crumpled Penny's face at his last words. *Kid sister.* Is that really how he thought of her? But she hadn't time to reflect on this sudden and devastating insight. A group of riders was approaching through the mist. On seeing him, one of the riders waved her arm in the air and trotted closer. Penny took a few nervous steps backwards.

'Kurt.' The woman's clear voice reached them above the clomping of hooves. 'Hello stranger. Long time no see.'

Penny watched from a safe distance as Kurt stepped up to the horse and rider. From where she was standing, the horse was a black, dangerous giant. Great clouds of steam were blowing from enormous pink nostrils. He — or she — Penny couldn't tell which — let out a nicker of recognition on seeing

Kurt before dropping a huge head to paw the ground. Kurt reached up to give the horse a careless pat on the neck, risking life and limb as far as Penny could tell from her nervous position several feet away.

'Hey, Cass,' Kurt said. 'Good to see you. How you doing?'

The rider lifted the reins, controlling the horse in a swift, elegant movement. Tall, willowy, red hair and — Penny would have bet on it — knew how to throw a lasso. This was probably Kurt's dream woman come to life. Definitely not someone who reminded him of his kid sister, she told herself bitterly. She watched from her position of safety as the woman leaned nearer Kurt, controlling the horse's restless stamping with an easy twitch of the reins.

'I'm doing well,' she said, in a voice that carried far, despite her slight build. 'And how about you? We haven't seen you at the stables for ages.'

The woman reached down to pat Kurt's hand in a teasing way, her gloved fingers lingering just a little longer than necessary. Kurt lifted his hand from the bridle and took a step backwards.

'I've been kinda busy,' he said. 'I just bought a new house over the way, and this is Penny.' He turned and beckoned in Penny's direction. 'Penny's doing some work on the house. Penny, this is Cass.'

Penny lifted a hand in greeting, keeping her boots firmly planted a safe distance from the horse's hooves. Cass took in her muffled face and the hems of her jeans, still dusty from Kurt's cellar, and gave the briefest of nods, raising a neatly gloved hand before turning her attention to Kurt.

'So you've finally bought a house in Richmond? Fabulous. We'll be seeing a lot more of you, then?'

Kurt's head tilted in that measured way he had when he was considering something. 'Yeah,' he said slowly. 'I'm planning on stopping by the stables on Sunday. I've an idea I'd like to run by you.'

'Fabulous,' Cass said again, with a lilting laugh. One of the riders called to her, and she lifted a hand to Kurt in a wave, ignoring Penny altogether. 'Bye, then. See you next week.'

With what to Penny seemed a terrible stamp of hooves, she whirled the gigantic horse round and trotted off to join the rest of the group. Kurt watched her ride away.

'Great rider,' he said, looking after her.

'Is she?' Penny followed his gaze to where the horses were now beating a path over the tall, wet grass. 'I wouldn't know. She's got her horse pointing in the right direction, so I suppose she must be.'

Kurt laughed and turned to look at her quizzically. 'I guess you don't ride.'

'No.' Penny was beginning to realise how big the gulf was that lay between their two worlds. Having rarely left London's streets, she couldn't imagine what it must be like to get up on a horse. She tried to imagine the thrill of galloping through wide open spaces, but the whole thing was so alien to her experience that her imagination — usually so ready to fill in the gaps — failed her.

'Did you learn in Wyoming?' she asked.

'My mom taught me when I was just a kid. My real mom, that is.' On the spur of the moment, he added, 'I could teach you if you wanted.'

★ ★ ★

An astonished silence followed his offer. As soon as the words left his mouth, Kurt himself could hardly believe he'd spoken them. It was one thing to take a walk in the park with Penny after a morning's work. Offering riding lessons was something totally different. It would throw them together on a far more intimate footing. And yet Kurt found a large part of him desperately willing Penny to say yes.

He glanced sideways at her, but with

her face all covered up like that, her usually expressive features were hidden to him. The little that was visible of her cheeks was unusually pink, but that might have been the effect of the cold.

'I don't know,' she said. She brought her mittened hands together and twisted them. 'I think I'd be a pretty slow learner.'

'I'm a patient man.'

Kurt imagined how it would be, spending more time with Penny, the physical closeness that riding lessons would bring, and was filled with an unexpected longing for her to agree. But he was sensitive enough to know if he pressed her too hard, she would back off and refuse altogether. He slowed his pace, turning to look at her.

'Why don't you just give it some thought?' He gave her one of his rare smiles. 'You never know, it might even be fun.'

Penny nodded, but there was a constraint to her response, and she offered no answering smile. Kurt realised it was the first time since he was an awkward teenager that he'd been turned down by a woman. Maybe he had come to take their acquiescence for granted. He gave a wry, inward laugh at himself as he turned his footsteps back to the path. Being with Penny was proving a novel experience in more ways than one.

*   *   *

Penny squeezed herself into a seat on the tube. The doors slid shut, and the walls of the station moved slowly past the window, gathering speed before plunging into blackness. She caught sight of her reflection in the darkened glass and pulled her hat off crossly, stuffing it into her bag. A knitted bobble hat was something a kid sister would wear. *Kid sister*. She remembered Kurt's expression when he'd said that's how he thought of her, and she winced again.

Good job she'd had her head screwed

on when he'd offered to teach her to ride. Her first reaction had been to cry *Awesome!* And even now the most treacherous excitement coursed through her at the thought. Luckily her imagination stepped in just in time, painting a picture of reality for once, and she'd had the good sense to turn him down.

She took in the disappointed expression on the face of her reflection in the window.

'Don't look like that.' She frowned at herself. 'You know what will happen. You'll be helped into the saddle, and then you'll have to tag along behind Kurt and Cass, like their annoying *kid sister*. And that will just be painful torment, not fun at all.'

Her reflection looked back at her, dejected. 'Stop it,' she told herself sternly. 'He's looking for a wife. He already has a kid sister. And the more time you spend alone with him, the worse it's going to be when he finally tells you he's got engaged.'

Her reflection didn't look any better

at this lowering thought, so Penny looked away and studied an advertisement for hair restorer. How silly she'd been when she imagined Kurt was a cowboy. What did she think would happen — that he was some sort of hero, ready to sweep her off her feet and ride off into the sunset? Granddad had often told her not to pin her hopes on dreams, and he was right. Dreams hardly ever came true in real life. Not for most people, anyway.

She stared at the unfeasibly black hair of the man in the advertisement until the train slowed for her station.

★　★　★

Kurt lifted the bottle of white wine the waiter had left and made to pour his date another glass. She raised a ring-covered hand to wave him aside.

'No more, thanks. One glass is enough. Too many empty calories.'

He replaced the bottle on the table, wondering as he did so whether his date could maybe do with a few more calories, empty or otherwise. All through their meal Jemima had shown an admirable determination to preserve her stick-like figure.

They'd been introduced through the dating agency and met first for coffee, where Kurt had asked Jemima out for dinner. On paper they'd seemed just right for each other. Jemima was down-to-earth, mid-thirties, attractive, and with an interesting career in law. When Kurt told her what he was looking for in a relationship, she'd told him she admired his common-sense attitude.

'So you've been to Wyoming?' he asked politely.

'Yes, we visited Wyoming a while back,' she said. 'Me and some ex. We went for the skiing. It was fun.'

Fun. Jemima delivered the word as though travelling to Wyoming was like taking a trip to the mall. She managed to make Wyoming sound, well, bland, somehow. As though she'd been to better places. And from what he'd heard from Jemima so far, maybe she had. She seemed to have travelled the world, always in the company of some ex.

He watched her pick at her grilled chicken, and an image of Penny came into his head the first time he'd met her. He remembered her reaction when he'd told her he came from Wyoming. Her whole face had widened, her blue eyes deepening in shade in that cute way they did when she was excited about something, which was pretty often. Kurt smiled softly at the recollection.

'So, how about you?' Jemima asked, spearing another piece of lettuce. 'What do you find to do with yourself when you're not at White River?'

'I think I mentioned I'm moving to Richmond? Last weekend I had a girl over that runs an antique place off the King's Road. She's refurbishing the interior.'

'Oh, antique businesses.' Jemima

waved her fork in the air dismissively. 'All that overpriced tat. Shame I didn't know you before. One of my exes does interior design in Chelsea. He'd have sorted you out with something really stylish.'

Kurt was beginning to think Jemima was more down-to-earth than he particularly felt comfortable with. He poured himself another glass of wine and started again. 'I kinda liked her antiques. I guess they weren't all shiny and new, but they had a story behind them. Some of it was real interesting.'

'Hmm.' Jemima pushed the remains of her meal to one side. 'The only time I ever bought an antique, it turned out to have woodworm. Had to burn it in the garden.'

'Uhuh.' Kurt tried hard to think of something to say to this but failed. Maybe this date wasn't quite right for him. Jemima seemed to lack something. Some sort of . . . imagination.

He took another sip of his wine and found his mind wandering again. He wondered what Penny would be talking about if she were sitting opposite him and suddenly realised he missed her company. He let his mind dwell on this surprising fact for a few minutes and then shrugged inwardly. He missed his kid sister, too. It didn't mean anything. He turned his attention to his steak.

* * *

Kurt had found himself thinking of Penny surprisingly often during the course of the week, and when Saturday finally arrived he gave a sardonic grin as he pushed open her shop door. If someone had told him a few weeks ago that he'd be looking forward to a day spent going through invoices, he'd have told them to go suck on a lemon. But the strange thing was he was relishing the prospect of spending time with Penny in her shop. She had a way of making everything seem fun — a quality Kurt's date had singularly lacked.

By the end of their meal that night, it had been obvious to both Kurt and Jemima that their relationship was not going to progress. Kurt tried a few avenues of conversation, but none of them had raised a single spark. During the course of the evening he had become increasingly taciturn. They parted cordially enough but with relief on both sides.

Although Kurt arrived at the shop bright and early, Penny was already behind her desk, talking on her mobile in a worried way. She lifted her head when she saw him and gave such a wide smile he blinked. Then she dropped her eyes quickly and finished off her conversation with a few rapid words before jumping up to greet him.

'Hi, you really came,' she said.

'Well, of course. We had a bargain, right?'

'Yes, well . . . ' She waved her hands uncertainly. 'I thought something more important might come up.'

'This is important.'

'Well, I'm really glad you're here.' She was smiling up at him with eyes that positively glowed. Her delight spread a delicious warmth through Kurt. Was she really so pleased to see him? He felt a ridiculous surge of happiness at the thought.

'I'm glad you're here,' she said again, moving a hand in the direction of her desk. 'There's a lot to do. I'm so grateful.'

*　*　*

Penny found herself gabbling out her words. She was madly happy to see Kurt again and trying not to show it. She turned to her desk and began systematically pulling out the relevant files, trying to hide her over-the-top response to his appearance behind a façade of cool professionalism. Her attempt at creating a distance between them obviously succeeded, because when she turned her head to glance at Kurt, she found the smile that lit up his eyes on seeing her had disappeared. He looked over to her desk and gave a cool nod.

'You'd better tell me where to start.'

Penny had filed every relevant document she could find in chronological order, going back the previous twelve months. She'd also opened up the business software on her laptop, all ready for Kurt's inspection. Now she lined everything up for him and went through it all as efficiently as she could.

Kurt sat in her usual chair whilst she stood behind, pointing things out on the laptop. She looked down at his dark blond head as he examined the files. After the initial warmth of his welcome, Kurt appeared to have retreated behind a professional exterior. In fact, as soon as he was in front of the accounts, he took on so much of his persona of head of White River that Penny felt almost intimidated. She could hardly believe that the man clicking rapidly through her computer files with such a forbidding expression on his face was the same man who had walked with her so companionably through the park the previous weekend, chatting and teasing her.

She stood behind him for a little while, feeling suddenly shy. After handing him all the documents, there really wasn't much else she could tell him, apart from the one thing that was worrying her. She cleared her throat.

'Kurt?'

He twisted round, lifting his head to look at her. 'Uhuh?'

She put one hand on the back of his chair. 'It was David on the phone just now, just when you came in. He's been phoning pretty often. Says he wants to come in and talk.' Her fingers gripped the chair back. 'I just thought I'd better let you know. Just in case he turns up suddenly.' She took a deep breath. 'Sometimes he loses his temper.'

The expression on Kurt's face hardened. Penny couldn't blame him. She thought it was only fair to tell him her ex-business partner was still on the scene. It would give Kurt the opportunity to walk away if he wanted. After all, it was one thing accepting Kurt's help with the accounts. Letting him get involved with a potentially aggressive ex-business partner was a different matter altogether. She scanned his face anxiously.

'No need to worry on my account,' he said.

Penny gave him a wide, relieved smile. It was strange how she felt she could trust Kurt after only this short time. His grey eyes were looking back at her steadily. Nothing she'd said appeared to have fazed him.

Penny tried to imagine what would happen if it actually did come to a confrontation. David was smaller than Kurt and a few years older, but he had a wiry strength and a pent-up aggression which he'd had difficulty in controlling in recent months. Despite his age, he retained a boyish charm which he put to effective use when talking to customers. There was no denying he'd been an asset to the shop in the past, but in recent weeks he'd undone all that by his outbursts of temper. Penny no longer trusted him. Kurt, on the other hand, had a reassuring solidity. If David did appear, Kurt would know exactly how to handle the situation.

Penny removed her hand from the back of his chair and gave a grateful smile. 'Thanks,' she said. 'I've been worrying about this so much. I keep trying to put David off, but I'm not sure how much longer I can keep it up.'

Kurt tilted his head. 'Yeah, I've been thinking about that. Maybe it's best if you don't let David anywhere near the shop. At least, not until I've gone through all of this.' He indicated the spread of files on the desk. 'Think you can hold him off for a bit longer?'

'I'll try.'

The shop's bell jangled, letting in her first customer of the day. Penny was about to head for her position behind the counter, but Kurt caught her hand, halting her for a moment.

'Any trouble, you let me know. You don't have to handle this alone. Understand?'

She nodded, looking down at their joined hands. His fingers were warm and comforting on hers, and it was tempting to return the pressure of his clasp. The shop bell rang again. For a few seconds, she let her fingers lie where they were, and then she slipped them loose and turned away.

★ ★ ★

After she'd gone, Kurt dropped his gaze to the files on his desk and then, on a sudden impulse, swivelled his head to examine the window where Penny had shown him the antique jewellery on his first visit. He could just make out the pearl and silver love token, still hanging in its place on the last peg. The morning light was streaming through the window, and the pearls gleamed faintly against the black velvet cloth.

So Penny still hadn't sold her pendant, which meant she still hadn't found someone who loved passionately enough to deserve it. The thought brought a smile to Kurt's face, followed by an unaccountable feeling of relief. He whistled softly to himself as he turned back to the computer screen.

5

At mid-day Kurt closed the lid of Penny's laptop and leaned back in his chair. His worst suspicions regarding the accounts had been confirmed. Now it was just a question of collecting rock solid evidence. Penny was talking to a customer at the cash desk, and he glanced over at her with a sudden surge of sympathy. When he told her what he'd discovered, she was going to find the news difficult to accept, and so was her grandfather. But now wasn't the time. He would have to prove it beyond all shadow of a doubt, and to do that he would need to come in a second time to go through her bank records more thoroughly. In the meantime, he'd done as much as he could for the day. With a feeling of relief, he stretched his long legs under the desk. Penny's work-space wasn't built for his large frame, and he was cramped from sitting too long.

Throughout the morning, the need to stretch had given him a good excuse to break off and watch Penny at work, and his admiration for her had grown considerably. She had a gift for people and talked to her customers with a charming mix of thoughtfulness and enthusiasm. She also managed to fob off a couple of customers who wanted to buy the diamond and pearl love token, which brought a quiet smile to Kurt's face as he surreptitiously watched her in action. The first customer she'd denied was a secretary whose boss had sent her out to buy an anniversary present. Kurt completely understood in this case. He'd enjoyed watching Penny sympathetically steering the harassed secretary away from the love token towards a delightful butterfly brooch which, she persuaded her, was far more appropriate.

It took Kurt a little while longer to figure out Penny's issue with the second customer she denied. A young man, good-looking, athletic, and, in his designer jacket and stubble, he'd seemed to Kurt to have all the right romantic credentials. He'd watched Penny lead the sharp-dressed man to the jewellery case, persuading him to look at a gold chain inlaid with sapphires and ignoring his request to look at the pearls. The young man gave the love token a long, lingering look before finally allowing Penny to charm him, and in the end, he left quite happily with the sapphires she'd picked out.

Penny gave Kurt an unrepentant grin after she caught his raised eyebrows. Later, as she was passing his desk, she stopped to offer him an explanation.

'I had to do it,' she said, jerking her head in the direction of the pearls. 'That guy'll be out of love with his girlfriend and in love with someone else before the year's over. I know it.' She took in Kurt's expression and folded her arms. 'I just couldn't let him have them.'

Kurt shook his head in mock exasperation. 'You're wasting a good sale.'

'I'm not selling them until it feels right.' She was walking away, when she halted and said over her shoulder, 'And one day the right man will come in. Someone who's actually in love, for once.'

Tehmeena caught the exchange and later stopped at Kurt's desk on her way to the cash till. 'Penny will never sell those pearls to anyone, you know.'

They both glanced over to the window, where Penny was demonstrating one of the mechanical toys. Tehmeena gave Kurt a conspiratorial smile. 'She's an incurable romantic.'

'Yeah, she sure gets passionate about things.' Kurt watched Penny lift out a set of three mechanical pigs and wind them up with a tiny key. When she set them down, the pig in front began playing the drums and the other pigs marched along behind, all three taking tiny, mechanical steps to the tinny beat.

A little group gathered to watch, and there was a burst of laughter. Kurt smiled to himself.

He was still gazing in Penny's direction when Tehmeena broke in on his thoughts. 'Why don't you ask her out?'

'What?' Tehmeena's question hit him like a bull out of nowhere, and he straightened in his chair.

'Ask her out.' She gave him one of her mischievous smiles and put her head on one side, ignoring his stunned expression. 'Ask her out for lunch.' She gestured to the clock on the wall. 'It's twelve o'clock. What did you think I meant?'

With a flutter of her eyelashes she wandered off to the cash desk, giving Kurt an airy wave and leaving him considerably thrown. He'd guessed how much of a friend Tehmeena was to Penny. She had soon demonstrated her vivacity and her lively sense of humour, teasing Kurt in a light-hearted way that he enjoyed. As the boss at White River, none of his staff would have dared *take the mickey out of him*, as the British put it. Even his own sister didn't really tease him all that much. The gap in their ages meant she treated him more like a father figure. So he liked the way Tehmeena bantered with him, making him feel at home, but then she had caught him totally off guard. Was she really hinting he should ask Penny out? He cast another glance in Penny's direction. Ask her out as on a *date* out?

Kurt picked up the remaining papers on his desk and began shuffling them until he realised he had no idea what he was doing. He replaced them in a heap then looked over again to where Penny was now replacing the toys. The pencil skirt of the first day they met had gone. Today she was wearing a vintage cream dress in some floaty type of fabric, and as she bent over to lock the cabinet, she was presenting him with a view he felt he had no right to be enjoying. He looked away hastily. With every movement she made around the shop that morning, the dress had flowed with her, draping softly over her breasts and hips and drawing Kurt's eyes far too frequently from the files in front of him.

Penny turned round to find his eyes had returned to her, and he stood up quickly, reddening a little under his tan. All of a sudden, he felt gauche.

'Finished?' she asked.

'Yeah.' He watched her approach, her dress clinging to her thighs with each step, and he lifted his hand to the back of his neck, rubbing it nervously. 'That is, no,' he added.

For a couple of minutes, Penny stared at him whilst he busied himself with straightening the folders on the desk. Then he cleared his throat and turned to her, gesturing towards his papers.

'I've been through all the files for the past twelve months,' he said. 'The good news is the figures basically look pretty healthy to me. Your cash flow should be picking up by the end of the month.

That is, if you can hold your creditors off for that long and put off spending on new stock for now. If the worst comes to the worst, I can pay you up front for the job in Richmond. That should definitely tide you over.'

Penny nodded with relief. 'That's great. And the bad news?'

'Something doesn't add up. Nothing to worry about for the moment,' he added, seeing the look of concern on her face, 'but I'll need to come back for at least another morning. And I'd like to check your bank records.'

'Oh?' Penny searched his face. 'Well, OK,' she said, puzzled. 'I'll organise all the paperwork for next Saturday. Thanks so much.'

'No problem.' He bowed his head, and Penny smiled widely.

'How about lunch?' she said. 'On me this time.'

'Yeah, Tehmeena thought I should . . . ' He broke off in confusion and shifted a couple of the papers on the desk. Penny gazed at him in astonishment. He cleared his throat for the second time. 'Tehmeena said it was about time I took you for lunch.'

She continued to stare at him for a little longer. Kurt knew he was behaving oddly. He tried to relax, to let go of his stiffness, and managed a small smile.

'There's a sandwich bar round the corner. It's a little walk from here if you fancy a change?'

'Great. I'll just go tell Tehmeena.'

Five minutes later they were outside.

'Sunshine,' Penny cried. 'Who'd have thought it?'

Kurt looked down at her and smiled. Now he was outside in his preferred element, he felt more able to relax.

'Yeah, sunshine. It's *fabulous*,' he said. 'See, I'm talking British already.'

'Spoken like a native.' Penny looked up at him with a happy smile, as pleased as he was to be outdoors.

They walked along companionably for a while, crossing the busy streets and threading their way past other pedestrians. Occasionally, Penny would point out a landmark, and, prompted by Kurt, she began to fill him in on a little of the area's history. He let her speak, saying little himself except to throw in the odd remark. His eyes were warm when they rested on her, and there was a quiet smile on his lips as she made the ordinary buildings come to life. She told him a pub on the corner had once been a police station. They peered in through the window and saw the desk sergeant's counter, now a busy bar thronged with lunch-time drinkers. An old blue police lamp still hung outside.

The next building they passed was a drab department store. Kurt had thought it nothing remarkable until Penny drew to a halt.

'This was the first shop in the whole of London ever to have electric light. Can you believe it?' She stared at the massive array of electrical goods in the window. 'Can you imagine how exciting it must have been? Oh.' She looked up at him, her quick mind jumping to another subject. 'That reminds me. I need to get more batteries for my camera. I'd like to take some photos of your house tomorrow. Do you mind if we go inside?'

'Sure.'

Kurt remained on the ground floor, examining the endless ranks of television sets, whilst Penny made her purchase as quickly as she could. She returned from the camera department to find him gazing in deep abstraction at one of the larger screens. She came to a halt. His arms were folded. Even from a distance his large, muscular body made a striking figure. He had the uncanny ability to remain absolutely motionless and, at the same time, give the impression of a vital physical presence. Penny stood for a while, unnoticed, wondering what on earth was on the screen that could cause such intense absorption. Then she smiled and shook herself. Sports was her guess. Probably American football. But when she rounded the aisle to stand beside him, she took one look at the screen and felt her heart come a stop with an almighty lurch, and the smile vanish from her face. This was no football match. It was an old romance, and the scene in front of her was playing out with sickening familiarity.

She looked up at Kurt. 'I'm back,' she said loudly. 'Shall we go?'

He didn't move. His eyes were still fixed on the screen, where a young girl stood outside a theatre, watching the crowds make their way up the steps. She was wearing a cream dress in some floaty material. She was slimmer than Penny, but the dress clung to her in much the same way. When she lifted her arm to wave to a man in the crowd, the similarity in the graceful movement was uncanny.

'Did you ever watch this movie?' Kurt asked without turning.

There was a short silence before Penny replied. 'Yes. It's *Queen's Act* with Megan Rose.' Her mouth was dry.

'It's the first film she ever made.'

Penny's mother was in her early twenties when the film was shot. Penny's father had been her agent. In the film she played the part of a struggling actress in one of London's theatres. Megan Rose's fans knew it as the film that launched her career and catapulted her to Hollywood fame. For Penny, the film had a far different meaning. It was the film that brought separation from her parents, eventually forever.

'My mom saw all Megan Rose's movies.' Kurt's eyes were still on the screen. 'She loved her. Thought she was so glamorous. She once bought a navy jacket because she'd seen Megan Rose wear one.' Kurt smiled softly at the stirred-up memory. Then he turned to look at Penny. 'Funny, though, I don't remember ever seeing this movie.' He looked back to the screen, where Megan Rose was now tripping lightly up an empty staircase, and then turned his eyes once more to Penny, searching her face for a moment. An expression almost of surprise crossed his features. 'I never thought of it till now, but has anyone ever said you look like Megan Rose?'

Penny stiffened. She could see Kurt's expression change from mild surprise to one of astonishment at her reaction. She thought briefly about turning on her heel and leaving without answering, but knew that to run away was out of the question. In any case, it would only raise more questions. She turned to examine the television set, which was suddenly filled with her mother's face lit from beneath so that her lips were dark as rowan berries, and her beautiful eyes glittered in the neon light from the theatre.

'No,' she said, the dryness catching in her throat. 'Of course no one's ever said that to me. Like your mum said, Megan Rose was glamorous, and she was beautiful.'

Kurt lifted his head in amazement. Penny turned to go, but he caught her arm. 'Please don't take offence,' he said quickly. 'I know your faces are different, but believe me, you look like her.' He dropped her arm, suddenly embarrassed. 'I just mean, you have a beautiful way of moving and speaking. She reminds me of you.'

The screen went blank before cutting away to a strident commercial. Penny stared at Kurt. She opened her mouth and took in a breath as though about to say something then changed her mind.

'I think I should be going.' She turned away. 'Tehmeena will be waiting.'

Their walk through the streets was a silent one. Penny was lost in thought, and Kurt kept looking at her, puzzled. When they reached the sandwich bar, her footsteps slowed.

'I think I'll just get something to take away,' she said. 'It's getting late.'

'OK.' He shrugged uncertainly.

The queue inside was short. Penny bought the sandwiches then they stood outside on the pavement, Kurt preparing to make his way in the opposite direction, back to the company flat he was occupying. He cleared his throat.

'So, what time you headed to my house tomorrow?' he asked.

'In the afternoon. I gave your team of decorators some instructions, and they've already made a good start. I just want to check on what they've done this week.'

'OK. Will I be in the way if I come over?'

Penny had to smile. 'Of course not. It's your house. I'd love you to see what they've done so far. But I thought you told Cass you were going riding tomorrow?' There was a tentative lilt to her question as she searched his face.

'Yeah, I planned on going to the stables, but only to talk with Cass and the head guy. There's something I want to discuss with them.'

'Oh.' Penny gave him half a smile. 'Cass will be disappointed if you don't ride with her.'

Kurt caught her look and grinned back. 'Yeah, she's always bugging me to ride. Trouble is she wants me to talk as well.'

Penny laughed with him at that, the image of the taciturn Kurt being forced to chat causing her eyes to light up briefly. Then the shuttered look came down again. She looked down at her feet for a moment before lifting her head to give him her clear blue gaze.

'Thanks for all your help this morning,' she said. 'I'd better get back.' He was about to say something, but she rushed on. 'I'm sorry about just now when you were watching the film. I've thought about Megan Rose a lot and why we're not alike. In fact, I've thought about it pretty much all my life.' Her eyes widened, glistening suddenly. 'You see, I don't tell many people this, but Megan Rose was my mother.'

She registered the widening of his eyes and stood still for a moment, uncertain. Then she swivelled on one swift heel, not wanting to witness the rest of his reaction, and made a craven escape through the crowds. She didn't stop until Kurt was out of sight. When she had rounded a corner she leaned back against a wall and breathed out deeply, ignoring the curious looks of the passersby. She found the fingers clutching her sandwich were trembling.

'This is ridiculous,' she told herself. She closed her eyes and pressed her fingers to her forehead. 'There, I've told him.'

Yes, she'd told him, but she'd been too chicken to hang around to see his reaction. Too scared to watch him make the comparisons and for the inevitable look of incredulity to cross his face. Kurt had noted the similarity between herself and her mother. Fine, there was bound to be something there. But he had told Penny that their features were not at all alike, and that was the truth. Ever since Penny was a schoolgirl, she had known her mother had been beautiful, and she was dull and ordinary. Her fellow pupils had pointed it out often enough, and Penny, already feeling the burden of not being able to replace her mother in her grieving grandmother's eyes, had been at too low an ebb to take her school-friends' taunts for the jealous barbs they were. It had been hard being made to feel second-best to a mother who was no longer there to make her feel good about herself.

She thought of her mother's face as she'd just seen it on the television screen: wide, luminous green eyes, and perfect creamy skin over her fine bone structure. On screen her mother's image had a romantic, ethereal quality far removed from Penny's solid presence. Penny was only too aware of the difference and knew only too well how much she had secretly disappointed her grandmother by not being Megan Rose, the fairy-tale film star who had died and left them.

She pulled herself away from the wall and set off back to her shop. Friends like Tehmeena knew the truth about her parents and barely remarked on it. Of course, David had known and had come out with all the comments she'd heard during her schooldays. *Hard to believe. You're so different.* That was one of the milder ones. The worst was the one he'd flung at her on the day he'd left: *You run this shop like an amateur because you're ridiculously romantic. You've got to realise life isn't like one of your mother's films. You're not your mother, and you never will be.*

Penny ignored the lump in her throat and carried on walking.

* * *

The sky was pale blue over Richmond Park, like the wash of a watercolour. Penny stood in Kurt's freshly painted living room, gazing out of the sweeping windows. She had pulled one of the panes ajar to let some air into the recently painted room, and now the spring breeze, sharp and cold, was drifting inwards. A thrush was singing in the branches of a tree, but although Penny's head was turned to the sound, her mind was far way. She was so wrapped up in thought she failed to hear Kurt enter the house. When a floorboard creaked behind her, she turned with a start. He was standing in the doorway, gravely watching her.

'Hey,' he said.

'Hey.'

They stared at each other. Penny was only too conscious of the abrupt way she had ended their conversation the day before. She had spent a troubled night wondering what Kurt would make of her disclosure. Now she waited for him to speak, but his mouth was closed in a grave line. He drew his hand from behind his back and brought forward a tissue-wrapped cluster of tulips. The red and cream of the flowers brought instant life to the chill room.

'I got you these,' he said simply.

'Oh.' Penny stepped forward, a sparkle leaping to her eyes. 'You didn't have to — ' She broke off, her eyes meeting his uncertainly above the colourful flowers which he was holding out to her with surprising gentleness.

'I felt bad about upsetting you,' he said. 'Going on about your mom and all. If I'd known how much it would upset you, I never would have said anything.'

'Oh, Kurt, it wasn't your fault.' Penny stepped forward to take the bunch of tulips from his hands and lifted them to breathe in their scent. 'If anything, it was my fault. I should have told you before, only . . . ' She looked down at the tulips, at a loss how to carry on. It seemed the normally taciturn Kurt would have to be the one to fill in all the gaps.

'Only you don't like strangers knowing. You've had to grow up in your mom's shadow, and you think people make comparisons. You think just because you're not your mom, people are disappointed in you.'

Penny's cheeks began to fill with

145

heat. In a few sentences, Kurt had expressed everything. She could hardly believe his astuteness or the gentle way he was speaking to her.

'Penny, your mom was beautiful, and she was famous, but what I told you before is true.' He held a hand out in quiet emphasis. 'You're not your mom. You're a real person, and you're unique. You've got a true heart and a beautiful way of moving and speaking. Hell, I could watch and listen to you all day.'

Penny raised her eyes to his. 'That's a lovely thing to say. The loveliest thing anyone's ever said.' She gazed down at the tulips. 'And thank you so much for the flowers. They're lovely, too.'

Kurt stepped a little closer and took hold of her chin.

'Don't mention it,' he said seriously. He bent his head, and for one brilliant, heart-stopping moment, Penny thought he was about to kiss her lips. Then his head moved to one side, and she felt his warm lips brush her cheek. 'I'm glad you like the tulips.' He stepped back. 'They're my sister's favourite.'

Her heart gave a sickening lurch, and she went still, gazing at the flowers held lightly in her hands. Of course tulips were a sister's sort of flower. Not roses or anything romantic like that. Of course not. Roses were the sort of flower a man would give to someone like Megan Rose, not her. She kept her head bent over the blooms for a while then lifted her chin to give him a faint smile.

'You're a good brother,' she said. Before he could say anything in reply, she changed the subject quickly. 'So what do you think?' She stretched out a hand to take in the room. 'I asked the decorating guys to start with your living space.'

It was the perfect change of conversation and helped take Penny's mind far from his kiss and roses and any of the other romantic dreams which otherwise would have swamped her head.

The rest of the afternoon was spent in going through everything Kurt's team of workers had achieved so far. In just a week they had wrought several changes, and Penny showed Kurt round with an air of pride. The living area was totally revamped. Previously wallpapered with a heavy embossed paper, the room had now been painted palest oatmeal, offset with areas of light, leafy green. The lightshades, which were 1930s biscuit-coloured glass, had been cleaned and replaced. The floorboards had been stripped, ready to stain in pale oak. The whole effect was to emphasise the magnificent greens in the parkland view from the window. Penny indicated this to Kurt, but he merely nodded, scanning everything with his usual keenness.

Major inroads had also been made on the rest of the house. The depressingly dark hall and stairs were now a brilliant white, and Penny intended to make good use of the space with wall-hangings. After the workmen had completely finished, the stairs would be carpeted with an old-fashioned runner, held in place with the existing brass stair-rods.

The kitchen and main bathroom had also been stripped, ready for refurbishing.

'And I've asked one of my restoration contacts to come in and clean up the old range in the cellar. He's actually quite excited about it. Says they don't come to light very often.'

'Guess not,' Kurt said, looking down at her, his grey eyes teasing. 'Guess most people would have thrown that old thing out years ago.'

Penny tapped his arm good-naturedly. 'It's going to look lovely. Wait and see.'

'Uhuh. Just don't blame me if the place is crawling with spiders.'

* * *

Penny gave a shudder and laughed. Some of Kurt's tension left him. It had pained him sorely to see her so unhappy. And it pained him even more that she had waited so long before trusting him enough to tell him about her mother. What did she think? That he would laugh in her face and say, Megan Rose's daughter? An ordinary girl like you? No way.

If anyone had told Kurt that ordinary was exactly how he'd thought of Penny the first time he'd seen her, he would have been incredulous. In the weeks that had passed since then, he'd totally forgotten there had once been a moment when he'd thought Penny ordinary to the point of plainness.

Penny lifted her head when they reached the bottom of the stairs and gave him one of her wide, delightful smiles, and in Kurt's eyes, everything about her just then was adorable. He reached a hand towards her.

'Come and take a walk in the park with me before you go,' he said on a sudden impulse. 'I still need to stop by the stables. You could come, too.'

Penny's eyes lit up, and he could have

sworn she was about to say yes. Then something must have occurred to her. The light died from her eyes, and the guarded look returned.

'That would be nice but . . . ' She hesitated, stumbling over the next words. She was so poor at dissembling, Kurt would have laughed if he hadn't felt such a wave of disappointment. 'I need to get back. I haven't spent much time with my granddad this weekend.'

Kurt regarded her without speaking for a moment. He knew there was something not quite right, something that Penny was holding back from him, but he couldn't place what it was. He thought about pressing the point, trying to get her to open up, but the shuttered look had come over her face again, and he merely nodded, resigned.

'OK. So I'll be back to look at your accounts next Saturday.'

Next Saturday sounded like an awfully long time not to see each other. Kurt and Penny looked at each other, the same thought going through their heads simultaneously, but neither of them speaking it aloud. Kurt was the first to move.

'Let's go,' he said. 'Time you were at home.'

★ ★ ★

Kurt clicked open the profile linked to the dating agency's site. Sara was a dance teacher living in London. She had two cats, enjoyed going to the movies and theatre, and was a surfer in her spare time. The accompanying photo showed a laughing, sporty woman who seemed perfectly pleasant. All the women who'd got in touch with him seemed perfectly pleasant. There was nothing wrong with them, so what the hell was wrong with him? Why did he think they all had something missing?

When he tried to capture what that thing was — tried to put it into words — somehow he just couldn't figure it out. He had tried several dates already, but nothing came of any of them. Maybe it was time to try a different agency. Maybe that was the problem.

He sighed and clicked off the screen. He knew deep down another agency couldn't do any better. It was his approach that was wrong. There were millions of women in London. Really, how hard could it be?

He was about to leave his desk when Tehmeena's question popped into his head again, and he stared at the blank computer screen. Why don't you ask her out? The words had been going round and round in his subconscious ever since Tehmeena had first thrown him the question with her mischievous smile. The trouble was, every time he thought of Penny he saw ... He stopped. Saw what? No matter how many times he tried to fathom his feelings, he was still no nearer understanding. The trouble was Penny wasn't one of his accounting spreadsheets to be broken down into neat component parts.

An image of Penny came into his head unbidden. She was standing as he'd seen her in his house that afternoon, gazing out of the window, her back to him. He thought of how she had looked, how the jeans she'd been wearing clung to her lovely figure and the transparency of her shirt in the light from the window, and he closed his eyes.

He had no right to be thinking of her in this way since it was only too obvious his feelings were not reciprocated. Why else would Penny have turned down his invitation to go for a walk, using some lame excuse about her grandfather?

He stood up from his desk. What were his feelings anyway? Admit the truth like a man. He didn't have any feelings, he just wanted to sleep with her. And then what? Tell her she wasn't the long-term relationship he was looking for? Tell her he was looking for someone practical and sensible who made no demands on his deeper emotions?

No, Penny deserved something else. She was looking for romance, and a girl like her deserved to have the moon and the stars and everything else she wanted. Kurt knew in his heart he wasn't that person. Whenever he thought of expressing himself emotionally, of using the words Penny would expect to hear from a man in love, his mind's eye saw with perfect clarity where it would lead. He saw a picture of his father and the way his passionate expression of love had led to his tragic withdrawal from the world and his own children.

Kurt wanted a family, children of his own. He wasn't prepared to take the risk of that world shattering around them, as it had for him and Ann. Somewhere in London there had to be a woman who shared his realistic view. He clicked back his screen, reopening the file from the dating agency and then clicked it shut again, shoving the mouse to one side. Maybe he should put the whole dating thing on hold for a while.

Just until his house was finished and his mind wasn't clouded with other things.

Other things, a small voice in his head mocked him. He ignored the voice resolutely and left his desk.

6

Far from pining at home, Daniel Rosas had in fact been out that Saturday on a golf course, enjoying the spring sunshine. He spent a perfectly pleasant afternoon with his friends, and would have been astonished to hear Penny claim they hadn't seen enough of each other.

The following Friday was Penny's regular night out with her girlfriends, and Daniel was looking forward to a quiet evening in his own company, watching the sports channels.

Penny was perched on an armchair in their living-room, rapidly stitching a set of pearl buttons onto a 1960s cocktail dress. She had undone her usual ponytail in order to sweep her hair into an immaculate beehive, and her eyes were made up in a dark and smoky blue. The dress needed a revamp

— hence the frantic stitching — but nothing else in her wardrobe would do. She had pulled out every item she possessed and found nothing to wear that didn't make her look a total frump. For a while, she'd been quite cross. But then, a lot of things seemed to be making her edgy lately, and she couldn't seem to settle to anything.

'Granddad?'

Her grandfather looked up from his golf magazine. 'Yes, love?' There was a slightly guarded tone to his voice. Not for the first time, he wished there was another woman in the family for Penny to turn to. He knew Penny had plenty of friends her own age, but she needed someone more like a mother than he could be.

Penny carried on making her tiny stitches without looking up. 'You know I told you Kurt came into the shop on Saturday? To look at the accounts?'

Daniel nodded. The mention of Kurt made him feel even more uneasy. In his opinion, Penny mentioned Kurt far too often in conversation. He had begun to wonder recently if it had been such a good idea for Penny to accept Kurt's help. He couldn't for the life of him understand what motivated a man of Kurt Bold's standing to help Penny in her small shop — apart from the obvious ulterior motive, which didn't bear thinking about. Penny's grandfather was old-fashioned. It had even crossed his mind to ask to meet Kurt for himself in order to check him out, but he was conscious of the fact that Penny was in charge of the shop now, and he didn't want to interfere in her life. Besides that, it seemed Kurt's presence was keeping David well away from Penny, and that could only be a good thing.

'Well, Kurt said something strange,' Penny continued. She put down her needle and began to fiddle with the discarded buttons. 'And it was out of the blue. He saw Mum on a television screen, and he said we look alike.' Penny lifted her eyes to give her granddad a searching look. 'Do you think that's true?'

Daniel laid down his magazine. Is this what had been bothering her? Or was it merely the fact that it was Kurt who'd noticed the similarity? Once again, he longed for a woman's intuition, but Penny was looking at him expectantly. All he could do was what any other parent would do in his situation — open his mouth and hope he found the right words.

'I suppose it was clever of Kurt to notice.' He watched with dismay as Penny's eyes lit up. It pained him that Penny had grown up continually comparing herself to her mother and finding herself wanting. Her mother was still admired as one of film's great beauties, and the thought that a man like Kurt had seen some similarity between them obviously meant the world to her. Her grandfather could have let the conversation go at that, but that would have been the easy way out. He forced himself to say what he had been thinking for a long time.

'Penny, after your mum died, everybody put her on a pedestal. Even your grandmother. Your mum became somebody she never was in real life. The person she became didn't exist except in people's imaginations and on a film screen. It's not true that you look like your mother.' Penny's head bent, and she began picking at the stitches she'd just made. Her grandfather's heart went out to her. 'But you can't expect to be your mother. You're your own person. I told you, you're not second-best. You never have been, and I want you to promise me never to accept second-best from anyone.'

She lifted her head at that to give him half a smile. Daniel reached over and patted her hand. 'You're the best granddaughter anyone could want.' He lifted his hand to look at his watch. 'And I bet you'll knock them dead in town tonight — but shouldn't you be getting your clubbing gear on?'

Penny leapt up, scattering buttons. 'Is

that the time? And it's not clubbing gear, Granddad. That went out in the sixties.'

'What goes around comes around.' He indicated her cocktail dress with approval. 'And you look beautiful. Make sure you don't get chatted up by any strange men.'

Penny pulled a face and made a dash for her room.

★　★　★

It was a fun evening. Because the demands of the shop took up so much of her time, especially since David had left, Penny didn't get out as often as she would have liked. It made a change for her to get dressed up and relax with Tehmeena and the rest of her girlfriends. They met at an Italian restaurant, where they were all shamelessly flirted with by the waiters, and they laughed themselves silly and enjoyed a great time. Now they were standing on the pavement outside, discussing where next to go.

'Let's go to Belinda's,' someone suggested.

Tehmeena, always the liveliest of the group, chorused her approval. Penny stood back and held up her hand with a laugh.

'I have to get back,' she said. 'I've had too much wine already. Us shop-workers have to be up early on Saturdays.'

'Boo,' said Tehmeena. 'I'm getting up early, too, and we hardly ever go out together. Just one more?'

'Come on, Pen. We never see you.'

There were several loud cries of friendly encouragement, interrupted when one of the girls stopped to let out a sudden wolf whistle. The girls turned round as one to watch a dozen men, each dressed in formal tux and bowtie, making their way towards them on the pavement. They were a loud, cheerful bunch, and they returned the chorus from a group of pretty girls with exaggerated pleasantries. As they drew nearer, it was obvious from the accents that most of them were from the States.

The man in front caught sight of Penny as they passed, lifted his fingers to his lips and blew her a kiss. Penny gave him an embarrassed wave, and her friends erupted into giggles. The group of men passed by with a mixture of laughter and loud greetings until only one was left. He was standing quite still in the shadows, looking at Penny. Her heart missed a beat.

'Hey,' he said quietly.

She stepped forward. Her friends seemed to have fallen silent all of a sudden. Unless the rushing noise in her ears was drowning out all sound.

'Kurt.'

He looked devastating. A dark silhouette in the gathering gloom. And he was staring at her, eyes gleaming in the light from the street lamp.

'Do you two know each other?' One of the men from the group — the one who'd blown Penny a kiss — had returned and was standing in the road beside them, his eyes on Penny. There was a short silence before Kurt turned.

'Penny, this is Alex,' he said, performing the introductions with slow reluctance. 'And these guys are my colleagues from the States. They're over for an awards ceremony. Alex, this is Penny. She owns an antique shop in the city, and she's furnishing my house.'

Alex stood in the road, regarding Penny and Kurt in a speculative way which only increased her sense of awkwardness. With a reluctance that equalled Kurt's, she indicated the group of friends hustling behind her, agog.

'You already know Tehmeena. And these are some friends from schooldays. We were just — '

'We were just persuading Penny to come to Belinda's,' Tehmeena broke in. 'Why don't you come with us?'

Penny whirled round, astounded. It was supposed to be a girls' night out. No Men Allowed. It was so unlike

Tehmeena to break their unwritten rule that Penny stared at her in silent vexation, but Tehmeena merely returned her look with the blandest of cheerful smiles. In the babble of talk that erupted, somehow it was agreed by somebody — and then eventually by everybody — that the two groups should indeed join forces and head for the cocktail bar. Penny looked at Kurt in dismay, but he had turned away to say something to one of his colleagues.

'Sure am glad we fell in with you girls,' Alex said, swiftly taking the opportunity to step in beside Penny. 'Me and the guys were headed back for a quiet night in the hotel bar. And don't tell anyone I said this,' he lowered his voice and gave her a conspiratorial wink, 'but me and the rest of that bunch have got eight hours together on a plane tomorrow, and we're already sick of each other's company. I'm real glad we met up with you. You've saved our lives.'

Alex had boyish, open features and

such a mischievous grin accompanied his words that Penny couldn't help but smile back. Then she caught Kurt's eyes on them both. From the look on his face, he didn't share Alex's enthusiasm at their joining forces. He looked unhappy. Annoyed, even. But there was no time to puzzle it out, because the whole, chattering group moved as one, and the next minute Alex took her arm, and she found herself propelled firmly in the direction of Belinda's.

★　★　★

Kurt propped himself at the crowded bar and took another sip from his bourbon. The music was loud, but he didn't need to bend his head to follow what people were saying. He looked past Tehmeena to where Alex was deep in conversation with Penny. The music wasn't so loud a guy had to put his lips to a girl's ear, for example. If Alex's mouth got any closer to Penny's head, he'd be eating it. And what on earth were they talking about? Whatever it was, every time he bent his head to hers, she laughed in that cute way she had, lifting her chin, her eyes crinkling up at him. Didn't she realise what a creep that guy was around women?

He felt a soft touch on his shoulder and turned to find Tehmeena gazing up at him, a worried expression on her face.

'I'm just going to sit down.' She indicated a table where her friends and Kurt's were engaged in animated conversation. 'Are you coming?'

Kurt shook his head, feeling a little guilty. He knew he was acting like a bear. Tehmeena was probably sick of trying to make conversation with him.

'I'll be going on home after I've finished my drink.' He raised his glass. 'You go on ahead.'

'Well, see you in the shop tomorrow.' Tehmeena stepped up on tiptoe to kiss his cheek. She nodded in Penny's direction and added something else, but her words were lost in the mix of music and chatter. Kurt just smiled back. Tehmeena stood, staring at him anxiously for a while before turning to rejoin her friends.

After she'd gone, he took another swig from his glass, trying not to look in Penny's direction, but it was damned hard to keep his eyes off her. In the past week or so, he'd begun to think of Penny as pretty, but the way she looked this evening, pretty wasn't the word. No, pretty definitely wouldn't begin to cut it as a vocabulary choice. The only word he could find for her was hot. So hot that when he first saw her standing with her friends outside that restaurant, he'd stood staring at her like some sort of country goof. From a distance, he hadn't even realised at first it was Penny, with her long legs and her hair all piled up like a princess. She was wearing a short silver fake fur jacket and had some silvery diamonds in her hair that glittered in the streetlight. She looked a million miles away from the tired, ordinary girl he'd first met in her shop. Why had he never noticed until now she had legs like that? It was no wonder Alex had stopped to stare at her.

He glared at Alex again. What did a guy like that find to talk about incessantly? Penny caught his eye, and he glanced away quickly. Kurt had never been one for small talk and found bars such as this one a strain. Everybody just chattering, chattering . . .

He closed his eyes momentarily. If he were alone with Penny, now . . . If they were alone, with her in that short dress, he knew damn well he'd have other things on his mind than making small talk. He drained the rest of his bourbon. The ice did nothing to kill the heat that was eating through his veins. He felt a tug on his sleeve and found himself gazing into Alex's perspiring face.

'Where's Penny?' Kurt asked, glancing round.

'She's gone to the restroom.' Alex

twisted his head to see if any of Penny's friends were listening then lowered his voice. 'Dude, that girl is something, isn't she? Why'd you keep her such a secret?'

'She's no secret. Anyway what's it to you?' Kurt pushed his empty glass across the bar. He knew he was angry and tried to lighten his words. 'I mean, you're heading home tomorrow, aren't you?'

'Yeah, but come on. I'm over here twice a month. And a girl like that would add some fun to a lonely hotel room. Know what I mean?' He broke into a grin before catching Kurt's murderous expression and held up his hands. 'Hey, hey. Why the bear look? She said there's nothing going on between you two, so what's your problem? And not likely to, either, she told me. Those were her exact words. So there's no harm in me getting her cell number.'

Kurt pulled himself upright. 'Did she give you her cell number?' he asked, not bothering to hide his incredulity.

'Nah, but it's only a matter of time.' Alex swallowed the last of his Manhattan, missing the thunderous flash in his friend's eyes. Kurt and Alex had worked together a long time. Kurt liked the guy, but he knew only too well how many women Alex had on the go and in how many cities around the world. As far as Kurt was concerned, his friend could have as many women as he liked, but he was going to make damn sure Penny wasn't one of them.

★   ★   ★

Unaware of the seething emotions brewing in their corner of the bar, Penny was weaving her way a little unsteadily through the tables. She'd retrieved her fur jacket and was planning on saying her goodbyes. The evening hadn't ended as much fun as it started out. Although she'd enjoyed Alex's conversation — he was a wicked flirt and some of the things he'd said made her laugh out loud — she wasn't so naïve she didn't recognise a serial womaniser when she saw one. In any case, it was hard to enjoy an evening when every time you looked up, you saw an unfriendly pair of scowling grey eyes. She was starting to feel quite on edge and even a little cross.

She began doing the rounds of goodbyes with her friends, relieved the evening was finally over. She'd just given a final hug and a promise of meeting more often when she felt a warm hand clasp her elbow. Kurt was behind her. His expression hadn't lost any of its unfriendliness.

'I was just coming to say good-bye — ' she began.

'Fine. I'll help you find you a cab.

'Oh, but I haven't said goodbye to — ' Penny looked over in Alex's direction, but he had his back to the room and was ordering another couple of drinks at the bar.

'I'll make your excuses.'

Penny felt her arm firmly gripped,

with no way to wriggle out of it without causing an embarrassing scene. She looked at Tehmeena for support, but her friend just gave her an airy wave of the hand and a wide grin.

'See you in the shop tomorrow,' she called with a wink. 'Bright and early.'

So much for friends, Penny thought bitterly. The next minute she felt herself propelled quite inexorably up the steps of the cocktail bar and out into the silent street. Kurt acknowledged the bouncer's goodnight with a curt nod of his head.

Kurt by name and curt by nature. Penny was suddenly overwhelmed with the urge to giggle. The fresh air in the street outside was doing terrible things with the cocktails inside her head.

'I don't need a taxi,' she said, trying to tug her arm out of Kurt's grip as he manoeuvred her along the pavement. She wasn't happy with the way he'd propelled her out of the bar, and suddenly, it was vital to assert her independence. 'I'm quite happy getting the tube. The station's just round the corner.'

'Yeah? And how about when you get off the tube? I bet it's a dark walk to your home.'

Penny didn't say anything. She didn't want to admit it, but the walk from her tube stop to her front door always made her a little apprehensive at night. It was a quiet residential area, and the lack of nightlife made the leafy streets particularly creepy. Kurt was right to look for a taxi for her, and her silence told him so.

'See? You need to get yourself a cab. And besides, I'm not about to let you freeze to death on the sidewalk.'

'Pavement,' she muttered.

'What?'

'I said pavement. We're in London not New York. It's pavement.'

'Whatever,' said Kurt, his eyes scanning the street.

'I say tom-ah-toes, and you say tom-ay-toes . . . ' Penny started singing in a gently mocking, tuneful way that she was quite proud of until Kurt swung her round to face him.

'Are you drunk?'

She raised her eyebrows and swayed a little. 'Kurt, shall we just call the whole thing off?'

'You're drunk. Hell, if you were my kid sister, I'd be giving you one hell of a scolding right now.'

His words had the sobering effect of a bucket of cold water. There was a momentary frigid silence before Penny brought her face up close to his. 'Well I'm not your kid sister. Alex doesn't talk to me as though I'm a stupid kid sister. So stop going on about it.'

'I know damn well how Alex was talking to you. Why do you think I got you out of there?'

'You got me out?' Her eyes blazed, and she edged dangerously closer. 'I was leaving anyway. I might have had a couple of drinks, but I know how to look after myself. So stop treating me like your kid sister, because I'm not.'

Penny's eyes glittered with anger and something that looked suspiciously like tears. Kurt stared into her face.

'OK, OK.' He caught hold of her, and she flinched beneath his touch. 'It's just I know how Alex is with women. We go back a long way. He's my friend, and when I saw you with him, I felt responsible. I'm sorry, OK? I'm sorry if I seemed highhanded.'

Penny's breathing was still shallow and coming in rapid breaths, her chest rising and falling beneath the thin fabric of her dress. With his back to the streetlight, Kurt's face was in shadow. She could make out only his eyes, which gleamed with sudden heat in the dark mask of his face. His hands tightened on her shoulders, and she felt the warmth of his breath flutter across her lips. She began to tremble, and he pulled her into his arms.

'You're cold,' he said quietly, although her body was warm in his gentle embrace. He kissed the top of her head. 'Here, here's a cab coming.' He released her, holding her away from him with a jerky movement, and she stepped back unsteadily. He lifted his hand, and the car pulled in to the kerb. 'Let's get you home.'

The cab's headlamps lit Kurt's features with a cold, yellow glow, revealing a mouth set in a harsh line. A small lump formed in Penny's throat. He opened the cab door, and she stepped in, averting her gaze from his.

'I'll be at the shop tomorrow,' he said.

He gave her a small, reassuring nod and half a smile. Their gazes locked, and for an instant he lifted his hand as though to touch her cheek. She held her breath, and then he withdrew, stepping back swiftly to push the car door shut. The taxi pulled away from the pavement, and she saw him turn and depart for home, head down.

Penny covered her face with her hands. Her shoulders lifted and fell soundlessly. She felt as though she had been physically torn from Kurt's arms. She couldn't understand why — if everything felt so right there — instead of holding her and kissing her, as she had longed for him to do, he had pushed her away and sent her home. As if she really was his kid sister. And she had been so dangerously close to lifting her head to press her lips to his. She shut her eyes with a groan. How humiliating that would have been. Her imagination was only too quick to fill in the scene: the embarrassment that would have crossed Kurt's face, how he would have put her away from him and told her she should get home to bed, like a little kid. Like a little kid sister. She winced again.

If she were an actor, she would know exactly how the scene should play out. How the hero would sweep the glamorous girl into his arms. How his warm mouth would feel on hers, his hands, the heat of him under her fingers . . .

Penny dropped her hands from her face. That scene hadn't been for her. It was played by a different actor. It was played by someone poised, someone stunningly beautiful, someone who said all the right words and played the part Kurt wanted her to play to cold perfection.

Penny just wasn't right, and she knew it. The thought of having to carry on in the kid sister role was getting too much to bear, though, and she felt a feeling akin to dread at what the next few weeks might bring.

★ ★ ★

Penny and Tehmeena were both a little pale when the shop opened next morning. Penny had lain awake for what seemed like hours, and when she finally fell asleep she was haunted by dreams in which she'd won the starring role in a play. Each time she'd been massively excited. But no matter how many times she applied her stage make-up, each time she looked in the mirror, instead of a glamorous beauty she found she'd been made up as a schoolgirl in pigtails. She woke up several times in a cold sweat.

'So,' said Tehmeena, all agog. 'How did it go?'

Penny looked up from her cup of tea. 'How did what go?'

'You know. Last night. You left with Kurt.' Tehmeena saw the blank look on Penny's face and continued, aghast. 'Don't tell me you don't remember?'

'Of course I remember. I was stone cold sober. Well, pretty much,' she added truthfully when she saw the sceptical lift of Tehmeena's eyebrow. 'But there's nothing to tell. Kurt saw me into a taxi outside Belinda's, and we each headed home to our own beds.'

'Oh.' Tehmeena fiddled with her bracelet for a moment. 'I thought he might . . . '

'Well, he didn't. He looked pretty cross the whole evening, to be quite honest. And then he couldn't wait to hustle me home.'

Her friend eyed her doubtfully. 'That's not how I saw it,' she said. 'I thought — ' The shop bell jangled to announce the first customer of the day. Tehmeena turned reluctantly, but before moving away, she made time to whisper, 'I thought he was jealous of you and Alex.'

Penny stared after her, almost dropping her tea-cup. Jealous! A jealous lover doesn't tell you off for being drunk and bundle you into a taxi like a naughty kid. Tehmeena was suffering from Penny's own wishful thinking. She dropped her eyes to her desk and the day's post. As difficult as it was, she needed to concentrate before the shop filled with customers. Kurt would soon be arriving, and she still had to sort out her bank paperwork for him.

She picked up the first couple of letters. Invoices. Luckily, the shop now had enough cash flow to pay the most pressing. She laid the invoices aside and picked up the next envelope. It was hand-written and had no stamp. It had obviously been hand-delivered, and Penny had a good idea who by. She tore it open with a feeling of foreboding.

Penny, it said. *I may have left the partnership, but we still have business to finish. I will call in at the shop today (Saturday) at closing time. Please make sure you are there. David.*

Penny put the letter down with an anxious frown. There was something intimidating about receiving a letter through the door. As though David had been lurking. Why couldn't he just e-mail or phone like normal people? This was all she needed. She'd been trying her best to keep David away, as Kurt advised, but she couldn't hold him off forever. In any case, David was right. There were final odds and ends to tie up regarding dissolving the partnership, and he had every right to insist on following them through. It was just Penny sensed he was intent on causing some sort of trouble.

'Everything OK?'

Kurt. She looked up with a smile of relief. She hadn't realised until now how much she had grown to rely on his support. It wasn't until she saw the faint constraint in his face that the previous night and the way it had ended came flooding back. She felt her cheeks warm. She laid David's note down on the table and stood up.

'Hi,' she said shyly. 'Did you get home all right?'

'Yeah. How about you? You feeling chipper this morning?'

'Yes,' she protested. 'I wasn't drunk.'

He grinned, and Penny realised she was being teased. There was such frank humour and openness in his smile, she couldn't help but smile back.

'Well, maybe a little,' she conceded. 'Thanks for finding me a cab.'

'No problem.' He gave the courteous nod of the head that caused her stomach to backflip. Then his eyes fell on the paperwork on her desk and David's scrawled signature. He lifted his head, expression hardening. 'What's this?' he asked.

'David wants to come over after closing tonight. I've tried to hold him off, but at the moment, he's quite within his rights. The partnership isn't legally wound up yet.'

'Yeah, he has a point.' He furrowed his brows in thought for a moment. 'But it shouldn't be a problem. I've got all day here. That should give me plenty of time.'

'Time for what?'

Kurt didn't answer. He scanned her desk, abstracted. 'You got those bank details?'

Penny sensed he was back in Head-of-White-River mode. In spite of the casual jeans and T-shirt that moulded his frame, he had his professional, aloof hat on. She pulled out the files he'd requested and logged him on to the shop's banking system before leaving him at her desk, deep in concentration over her paperwork.

The day flew by. Saturdays were always busy, and the steady stream of customers kept Penny's thoughts from turning too often to the scene with David that lay ahead. Even so, she occasionally caught herself battling nerves. She disliked confrontation at the best of times, and her last conversation with David had been almost frightening. His towering rage and his accusation that she was too ridiculously romantic to run a business still played out in her mind, no matter how she tried to prevent it. From time to time she glanced over to her desk, where the sight of Kurt, handsome head bent in unhurried concentration, was a solid reassurance.

When the time finally came to lock up, Kurt put down his pen and lifted his arms above his head in a final stretch. Penny tried not to stare, bringing her gaze to somewhere round the stack of papers which Kurt had now organised into neat piles. Tehmeena had left for the day, leaving just the two of them. The shop seemed extraordinarily small. Penny approached Kurt's desk, and he stood, drawing his frame to its full height.

'Nervous?' he asked, looking down at her with such harshness in his normally warm expression that Penny stared and almost said yes but not for the reasons he thought. There was something in the way the muscles on his arms were flexed, bunched hard in a rigid mass that spoke of intense repressed anger. His normally impassive features were intimidatingly grim. She realised he was asking her if she were nervous of the coming confrontation, and she shook her head without speaking. All of a sudden, David's bullying was no longer something to be feared. With Kurt beside her, she felt she could face anything.

He softened and smiled briefly. 'Good,' he said. 'There's nothing for you to worry about.' He picked up his coffee mug from the table. 'Shall I make you a cup of tea? I guess that's the British answer to everything.'

He gave her a wide smile, relaxing his forbidding expression, and Penny nodded. She watched him disappear into their little kitchen just as David's silhouette appeared outside the shop door.

7

'So.' David picked up one of the files from Penny's desk and began flicking through the pages. 'You've got White River in to do your books. And how are you managing to pay someone like Kurt Bold for his services?' He swept Penny a glance that left her in no doubt of the way his mind was working.

Penny retreated behind her desk. How had her grandfather ever grown to trust this man? The mask of charm had fallen totally, and he was looming over her with a sneer and a hint of threat that she would have found frightening were it not for Kurt's presence in the kitchen.

'You're offensive, David. And it's none of your business, but actually, you're right. I am paying in kind,' she said truthfully, thinking of the work she had done on Kurt's house.

David's sneer deepened. 'He must be getting an excellent service.'

Penny didn't bother to rise to the bait. She lifted her chin. 'Let's just finish what we need to. I've made a list of the papers that will need signing and the money you're owed from the business. If you'd like to check through them, I'll have our solicitor draw up the documents.' She made for an envelope on her desk, but David caught hold of her arm in a tight grip.

'And what if I've changed my mind? This shop's been a nice little earner for me. Maybe I'm not ready to leave, after all.'

'You wouldn't,' she gasped. 'You can't stay here now.'

'Can't I? We're equal partners, remember? Maybe you're the one who ought to be leaving, not me. If I leave, you'll never make a go of it on your own. You've no head for business. You're a pathetic dreamer, Penny.'

There was the sound of a quiet foot-fall behind them, and the atmosphere in the room changed perceptibly. David said nothing, but his grip on Penny's arm loosened. He was breathing heavily. He stared into Penny's shocked face before releasing her arm and turning around.

Kurt was leaning against the far wall, arms folded.

'Guess you may want to think through what you just said.' He gave the words his usual slow, measured delivery. 'And I guess you owe Penny an apology. Guess you should take a look through those documents she gave you and think about what you need to sign. I draw the line at any money coming to you, though.' He pulled away from the wall and unfolded his arms, dropping them to his sides. 'Unless it's the money you owe Penny.'

David turned white. 'This isn't your business.' He turned to Penny. 'What the hell's this guy doing here?'

'Penny's business is my business.'

Kurt dropped his gaze to David's clenched fist, his only acknowledgement of it a slight narrowing of the eyes. 'Unless you'd like me to make it a matter for the cops,' he continued evenly. 'I'm sure if I tell them what I've found in those books there, they'll be happy to take it up.'

Penny gasped, and David's face flooded crimson. He reached forward impotently as Penny took several hurried steps towards Kurt, who caught hold of her and drew her to him.

'I'm sorry, Penny.' He looked over her head at David. 'Your partner's been stealing from the business for years. In your grandfather's day he was hiding his tracks pretty well, but once you took over, seems he got a little careless. But looks like he underestimated you. You guessed something was wrong.'

'Yes, but not this!' Penny stared at David, horror-struck. 'I never guessed he'd been stealing. How could you do this? How could you do this to

Granddad? After everything he did for you.'

David gave a short, contemptuous laugh. 'This shop was going nowhere without me. It was me who brought the biggest customers in. Your grandfather was bad enough, but you've got your head in the clouds. You'll never make a go of it without me.'

Penny's face felt tight and stiff.

'You've said enough.' Kurt didn't move. A terrifying coldness entered his expression. 'What did you think?' His eyes raked David contemptuously. 'That you could afford to get careless? Did you think Penny was too stupid to guess something was wrong?' He watched David's sneer falter and took a step forward. 'Time to call the cops.'

He stretched out a hand to where his phone lay on the desk, but Penny leapt for his arm with a cry.

'No.' She put her hand over his urgently. 'No, don't. Don't get the police in. It will kill Granddad.'

Kurt's eyes were hard on hers, his

arm unbending under her fingers.

'Think about it,' she urged in a low, quick voice. 'It will drag our shop's reputation in the mud, and worse than that, my granddad will be made to look a fool when he's just a generous, trusting man.'

Kurt said nothing for several seconds. He looked into Penny's stricken face for what seemed an age before lowering his arm slowly. He turned to David, his expression one of stony contempt. 'It sickens me to do this, but I'll make you a deal. You sign every damn paper Penny's solicitor sends to you. Then you never, ever set foot in this shop again. The day you so much as whisper a word to Penny or her granddad is the day I call the cops and have you slapped in jail for theft. Understood?'

David curled his mouth in an attempt at derision. 'I just took what was owed me. There's no way Penny can run a business. I told her, she's a pathetic romantic. She — '

'Get out.' Kurt didn't raise his voice. He stood perfectly still, but a terrifying sense of threat emanated from every inch of his solid frame.

David backed away, the sneer not leaving his face. The bell jangled as he pulled the door open, and he lifted his head to look one last time at Penny. 'Don't imagine this guy's interested in a nobody like you,' he said. 'Your mother was somebody. But you? You're nothing and nobody.'

'Get out.' Kurt moved forward with such icy ruthlessness that Penny leapt to clutch at him, to hold him back, but there was no need. The shop bell clanged furiously as it slammed shut. They listened to David's hasty footsteps retreating down the street, and then there was silence, broken only by the sound of Kurt's quick breathing.

Penny put her hands over her face. For a moment or two, Kurt didn't move, and then his strong arms enfolded her. She stood stiff and unyielding with her eyes squeezed shut beneath her hands. Kurt held her, pulling her resistant body towards him until her cheek rested on his chest.

'It's OK. It's all right now,' he said.

She felt his warm breath flutter over her head. She didn't speak. David's words were like physical blows. *Your mother was somebody, but you're nothing and nobody.* A rush of nausea swept over her, making her feel faint. She knew she should be stronger — should find the courage to stand tall and pull away from Kurt's embrace — but she was afraid that if she moved so much as an inch she would dissolve into tears. She thought of the years of contempt in which her grandfather's partner had held them both — years when they had shown David nothing but generosity and kindness — and the feeling of nausea strengthened and became so overpowering, she sagged against Kurt's chest.

'Here, come and sit down.'

She felt herself being pushed gently into a chair. She laid her head down on her desk and heard Kurt retreat into the kitchen.

Your mother was somebody. But you're nobody. The words pounded in her head with every beat of her pulse.

'Drink this.' Kurt gave her a gentle shake. He had returned with a glass of water. She lifted her head dizzily and took a few sips until the swimming sensation subsided, and she could try and pull herself upright.

'Take your time.' Kurt hunkered down beside her and took one of her hands in his. 'I'm sorry.' He was looking up at her anxiously. 'I never would have allowed him in the shop if I'd guessed. Was he always like this?'

'No.' Penny shook her head a little too vehemently, and the dizziness returned. She leaned back in her chair. 'No. When he first started working for Granddad, he was great. Always charming and chatty in the shop. No one would have guessed at this.' Her voice broke, and she took another sip of water, trying to control herself. 'But the whole time, he was lying in our faces. I don't know what I'm going to tell Granddad. He really trusted him.'

Her face began to crumple, and she felt Kurt tighten his grip on her fingers. She lifted her eyes to find him gazing over her shoulder at the door where David had just left, his expression so intensely grim she recoiled. He caught her movement and turned his head. Instantly, he softened.

'Don't worry,' he said, catching her shocked expression. 'I'm not going after him. But it would give me great satisfaction to give him the beating he deserves.' His eyes darkened, and he glanced longingly at the door. 'But I guess that isn't going to help you much.' He focused his gaze on her, relaxing his grip on her hand. 'You need to tell your granddad the truth,' he said.

She nodded. 'I know. If there were any way I could keep it from him . . . ' She wiped her wet cheek with her sleeve. 'But he has to know. We couldn't possibly hide it from him. But oh, Kurt

— he'll be devastated.' She raised her head, eyes blurred with tears. 'And then he worries about me so much. This will just make it worse.'

Kurt looked down at their joined hands and turned her fingers over in his, frowning. Then he gripped her hand reassuringly and looked up.

'How about I go with you? To tell your granddad, that is.'

'Would you?' Penny stared at him. 'You don't have to but . . . ' She left her sentence unfinished. Having Kurt to support her would relieve her of so much of the anxiety of breaking the news. Her granddad would stop worrying about her — or at least, wouldn't worry about her quite as much — if he thought she had Kurt's support.

Kurt heard her unspoken words and nodded.

'No problem. We'll go together.' He got to his feet and drew her up after him. 'OK?'

She nodded her relief. 'Thank you. Granddad's out tonight. With some friends. And I'm going to an auction tomorrow. How about if we speak to him tomorrow evening? You can stay for dinner if you like?'

'Yeah, that sounds good.'

They stood and looked at each other a little awkwardly. It sounded as though Penny had just given Kurt an invitation to meet the parents.

In a rush to break the awkwardness, she said the first thing she thought of. 'Shall I buy you a drink? I feel like I owe you one.' As soon as she'd said the words, the heat mounted to her cheeks. Now it sounded like she was asking him out on a date, for goodness' sake. And acting awkward made it seem even more of an issue, but the realisation just heightened her embarrassment.

Kurt looked equally ill at ease. 'Well, that would be great, but actually, I need to get going. I have plans for tonight.'

'Oh, of course.' Penny turned to tidy her desk as though their conversation were the most natural thing in the world. Of course he had a real date with a real girlfriend. He was still on his quest to find a wife — he didn't have time to waste socialising with Penny.

'And how is the dating going?' She cursed herself furiously. *How is the dating going?* What sort of an inane question was that? She carried on righting the files David had turned over, her mind whirling. On Monday morning, she would probably find out they were all in totally the wrong order.

Kurt cleared his throat. 'Actually, I'm not on a date tonight. I'm meeting Cass.'

She turned, brows raised in surprise. 'The girl we met out riding?'

He nodded. 'I'm sponsoring a charitable project. It involves the stables. Cass offered to help.' There was a hint of earnest emphasis to his explanation. 'It's kind of a business meeting,' he added.

'Sounds interesting. Hope it works out.' Penny accompanied her words with a smile that barely matched the emptiness she felt. 'Granddad and I will just have to cook you something special. It's the least we can do.'

She congratulated herself on her answer. It had just the right amount of cool friendliness. They spent the next ten minutes companionably shutting up the shop, and it wasn't until Penny was alone on the tube on the way home that she allowed herself the luxury of feeling miserable. In the space of an hour, she'd found out her business partner was a liar and a thief, she'd come on to a guy she was falling in love with and been given a brush off because he was meeting someone else, and now she was going home to pretend everything was fine to a grandfather who worried too much.

By anyone's reckoning, it had been a dreadful day.

* * *

Later that evening, Kurt saw Cass into a cab after their productive meeting and headed home to his apartment. It was a cold, clear night. As clear as it ever would be in London's neon-lit streets. It was at times like these he missed Wyoming. At this time of year, the sky arched over the plains, clear and heady, exuberant with stars whirling away into infinity. It was the sort of wildly romantic landscape which would appeal so strongly to Penny. He could imagine her, eyes wide with silent wonder, gazing up into the firmament. For a moment, he had an intense longing to be there beside her, sharing her wild joy in the night's rich landscape.

Then he looked down at the littered street and kicked an empty takeaway box into the gutter. He'd discovered the hard way that life wasn't all stars and romance. It was the only lesson his father had ever taught him. He'd watched his father reach for the stars, only to find them crashing around his ears, leaving him a broken man and his children shattered. Kurt had long since determined never to follow the same path. The arc of his life since leaving home had followed a safe, predictable trajectory. He'd worked hard in a sensible business, where the numbers he dealt in every day followed a totally logical pattern. Now he wanted to find someone to share that ordered life with him. But that someone would have to conform to his ideal, be happy to lead the same secure, predictable life at home as he'd forged for himself in the workplace. Not someone who made his heart leap uncontrollably whenever he saw her. Not someone who made him feel dangerously out of control as soon as his arms were around her.

Not someone who had fragile dreams of her own which he was in danger of shattering by acting selfishly.

His house would soon be ready to occupy, but other than that, he had fallen far behind in his ordered life plans. Trouble was, whenever he thought of the effort of getting back on the dating circuit and meeting other women, everything seemed flat and lacklustre. Maybe when he'd moved into his new house and Penny was no longer part of his life. Maybe then he'd be able to move forward.

He shrugged his shoulders against a sudden biting draught of wind and strode home, without looking up at the sky again.

* * *

Penny finished laying the dining-room table for Sunday dinner and took a step back.

'Lovely,' said her grandfather. He paused on the threshold to survey the freshly laundered tablecloth, the cutlery and glasses, all exactly aligned. 'But maybe you should move the flowers another centimetre to the left.' He looked serious, but there was a definite twinkle in his eyes when they rested on her.

Penny coloured. Her attempt not to give her granddad any idea how nervous she was about the evening had failed. He knew her too well. She'd fretted with slightly too much intensity over what to serve and whether to put out her mother's china service before finally deciding it would be better to be informal. An inordinately long time had been spent deciding what to wear. She had just changed out of a slightly too formal black dress to come downstairs in dark jeans and a blue cashmere top. Now, for the last ten minutes, she had fussed about arranging and re-arranging the dining table so that everything was to her satisfaction.

'I thought Kurt was coming over to discuss the accounts. Or does he have some other intentions I need to know about?' Her grandfather gave a mock questioning look over the top of his glasses. He was eying Penny in a way that made her feel even more ill at ease, if that were possible.

'It's just business, Granddad, that's all,' she said quickly.

Any further questioning was cut short by a strong, single rap on the front door that made Penny jump. She slipped thankfully from the room. When she pulled the front door wide, Kurt was standing on the step with a bottle of bourbon in one hand, loosening his shirt collar with the other. Penny's already quickening pulse took a leap. Only Kurt could wear a pale pink shirt and make it look masculine. He leaned forward, bringing with him the fresh scent of the evening air, and kissed her cheek.

'Everything OK?'

Penny glanced over her shoulder down the hallway. 'Yes,' she said in a low voice. 'I haven't told him anything yet, though.' She raised her eyes to his. 'Thanks for coming. It means a lot.'

'No problem.' Kurt dipped his head with the courteous nod which never failed to make her heart jump. Her grandfather appeared suddenly behind her.

'Come in, come in,' he called affably. 'Don't keep Kurt on the cold doorstep.'

Penny drew aside to let Kurt enter, and the two men shook hands.

Although Kurt's back was to her, she could make out an appraising look in her grandfather's eyes as they greeted each other. Daniel was tall, but Kurt stood a couple of centimetres taller, and he seemed to dominate their house as soon as he stepped over the doorstep. Penny's grandfather appeared satisfied with what he saw, releasing Kurt's hand with a small nod before leading the way into their sitting-room.

'What can I get you to drink?'

'I took the liberty of bringing you this.' Kurt proffered his bottle. 'Genuine Kentucky bourbon. I fetched it from the States on my last trip home.'

Daniel's eyes lit with pleasure. The two men fell into small talk on the merits of their country's respective whiskies, and Penny retreated to fetch a couple of glasses from the kitchen. A shot of bourbon might have helped clear her own nerves, but she decided against it. She needed to keep a clear head for breaking the bad news about David. Knowing Granddad, she doubted it would be long before he would want to bring the small talk to an end and get down to the real reason behind Kurt's visit.

Sure enough, once the bourbon had been tasted and appreciated, Daniel placed his glass on the side-table and put his hands on his knees, ready to get to the real reason for Kurt's presence.

But Kurt pre-empted him. His expression sobering, he leaned forward. 'I guess you want to know why I'm here.' He looked up at Penny, who tensed miserably. He gave her a reassuring smile before returning to Daniel. 'I wish we could have met under different circumstances, but Penny asked me to come here tonight to help her break some bad news.'

Penny watched her grandfather draw back. She bit her lip anxiously.

'I'm sorry to have to tell you this, but I took a good look through the shop's accounts, and there were a lot of anomalies that didn't stack up. I began to have serious doubts about your former partner's actions, and so I checked and double-checked, but in the end, there's no avoiding the truth. Your partner has stolen a considerable amount of money from your business.'

Daniel's face whitened, and Penny moved swiftly to his side. He stiffened and sat upright, waving her away.

'Are you absolutely sure of the facts?' His gaze met Kurt's steadily, despite the slight tremor in his voice.

Kurt nodded gravely. 'I wish I could say there was some doubt, but I'm afraid I have all the evidence I need.'

It broke Penny's heart to see her grandfather sink lower and lower in his chair. Kurt went through the steps he had taken to unearth David's theft, answering all the older man's questions calmly, going into details when asked but glossing over their final confrontation in the shop. Penny was more grateful to Kurt for his sensitivity towards her grandfather than she could ever express. He'd shown considerable tact and spared her granddad from discovering that, besides being a thief, David was also a bully. If her grandfather ever discovered the contemptuous way David had spoken to her, it would have hurt him far more than the fact that his partner had been stealing from him for years.

Penny rose quietly and went into the kitchen, leaving the two of them to talk whilst she finished preparing the meal. As she mixed together the ingredients for a salsa verde for their steak, Kurt's deep, slow voice drifted through from the next room, interspersed with her grandfather's occasional comment. Kurt had a collected, reassuring way of speaking.

Thanks to Kurt her granddad had taken the news far better than she had expected. She just hoped he would be able to eat after the shock of David's duplicity. She was just lifting the sizzling beef from the pan when the sound of laughter surprised her as it filtered through from the next room.

She put her head around the

sitting-room door. 'Dinner's ready.' She glanced from one to the other. Amazingly, Kurt seemed to have diverted her grandfather from the terrible shock, and they were both bursting with some secret amusement. It wasn't until she'd seated everyone around the table that they finally filled her in on the joke.

'Kurt's been telling me how you first met.' Daniel's eyes twinkled. 'I told him I already knew about the cowboy from White River story.'

Penny buried her face in her hands. 'Am I ever going to live that down?' she asked, her voice muffled.

'Well in a strange way, maybe you were right, after all, Penny.' Daniel turned to Kurt. 'Penny's very intuitive about people. You might be no cowboy, Kurt, but you certainly rode to our rescue with David.' He raised his glass in Penny's direction. 'So take no notice when people say you're a dreamer. You've got a rare gift for understanding people.'

Penny flushed warm with pleasure.

After all the terrible insults David had thrown at her, her grandfather's faith in her was like water on a parched rose. She beamed at him, her heart overflowing with tender affection.

* * *

Kurt looked down at his wine glass. What wouldn't he give to be on the receiving end of one of those smiles from Penny? But when he raised his head and their eyes met, instantly, just as he knew it would, a veil descended and there it was — that ever-present constraint when she looked at him. The pain her withdrawal caused was like a slice from a knife, but he kept his eyes steadfastly on hers. He raised his glass to her before turning to Daniel.

'You're right. Penny has a gift with people. And she makes her antiques come alive in that shop. I love to listen to her. Even though she refused to sell me her love token.' He smiled teasingly in Penny's direction whilst she rolled her eyes.

Her grandfather gave a laugh. 'Is she still holding on to that thing? It's been in the shop for months. So who's the right buyer, Penny? Do you think he'll ever show up?'

'I'll know him when I see him, Granddad.' Penny shook her head. 'I just haven't had a customer who's really in love yet.'

'Sometimes Penny gets attached to one of our antiques,' Daniel told Kurt. 'She won't let it go until she thinks it's right. And do you know, in a strange way, her regular customers love it.'

'I can understand that,' Kurt said. 'It sure worked with me. She's furnishing my whole house. I have total trust in her.'

For the first time that evening, Penny's reserve dropped. Her eyes glowed, and the smile she threw Kurt radiated warmth. He smiled at her as she leaned toward him, a rosy flush deepening in her cheeks.

Beside him, Daniel sank back in his chair, a thoughtful expression on his face as he glanced from one to the other. Eventually, he cleared his throat, and Penny dropped her gaze.

'So, Kurt,' he said affably. 'How is your house in Richmond progressing? Penny tells me you're getting married. You must be eager to get everything finished.'

Although Daniel's expression was amiable, there was a slight hint of steel in his words that gave Kurt pause. He answered with a little less than his usual composure. 'It's true. I'd like to get married some day. Start a family. But I'm in no rush. Fixing a house is a first step.'

'You're right not to rush it.' Penny's grandfather eyed him. 'Marriage is a serious step. An eligible chap like you must have broken enough hearts in your day without adding any more to the list.'

Kurt's hand stilled on his wine glass. He kept his gaze fixed steadily on the older man's. 'I don't aim to break any hearts. And in any case, I expect the woman who marries me will be level-headed enough not to have her heart broken, by me or anyone else.'

His gaze travelled to Penny. She was staring at her plate, eyes lowered, and her face looked pale in the light from the candle. Her grandfather said something, but neither of them replied. For a couple of seconds, there was a hush in the room.

Then Penny stood, pushing her chair back with a harsh scraping sound. 'Your house,' she said, turning awkwardly. 'What with David and — and everything. I completely forgot to tell you. I was at an auction this morning and bought you quite a lot of stuff.' She looked at him uncertainly. 'That is, I hope you don't mind? If there's anything you don't like, I'll keep it to sell in our shop.'

'Of course. I told you just buy whatever you need. I have total faith in you.'

The rest of the evening was spent poring over the auctioneers' catalogues. Daniel amused Kurt with stories of auctions he'd been to in the past and the triumphant buys, not to mention the magnificent losses, he'd made during the course of his career. It was a light-hearted, open conversation, and by the time Kurt stood to leave, some sort of ease had been restored between them.

Daniel stood to take Kurt's hand firmly in his. 'I can't thank you enough,' he said. 'Not just for what you've done for the business, but for the care you've taken of Penny.'

He pressed Kurt's hand again and a flicker of understanding seemed to pass between them.

'No problem.' Kurt nodded, returning his gaze steadily. 'And I hope to return your hospitality once Penny's finished work on my new house.'

'Yes, indeed. You must keep in touch once you're married.' Daniel turned to Penny. 'Isn't that right, Penny?'

'Of course,' she said.

Something in the way she spoke made Kurt turn his head. The stiffness in her expression caused his heart to sink.

'Once you're married, we'd be happy to visit,' she continued, all politeness.

But something in the emptiness of her gaze told Kurt that once his house was finished, she had no intention of stepping over the threshold ever again.

8

'I always knew David was a creep — but this! I can't believe he did this to you.' Tehmeena stared at Penny in horror. 'Pretending to be Mr Big with the customers when he'd been stealing from us all along.'

Penny nodded. She'd got out of bed that morning still feeling tired and worn, and not even the application of makeup could hide her pallor. 'If it hadn't been for Kurt, I would never have guessed. Well, not for a long time, anyway. And I just don't know what I'd have done if Kurt hadn't been there to confront him.' She shuddered. 'It was horrible.'

'I still can't believe it. And turning nasty like that. It's so lucky Kurt was there with you.'

Penny grimaced inwardly. Hard to believe it was only a matter of weeks since Kurt first walked into her shop. In that short space of time, she'd come to rely on him so much. Too much. Something desperately needed to be done about that. Kurt still intended to marry the right woman — someone *level-headed* as he'd made plain during dinner — and once he was finally married, he would have other priorities. Penny would only be getting in the way, like a kid sister tagging along. It was time to draw a line in the sand before it was too late.

'Kurt's been great.' She tried to make herself sound collected. Tehmeena was about to break in, but Penny turned the subject, afraid if her friend probed her feelings she would crack. 'Now David's gone, we're going to be really short-staffed. Maybe we should think about taking someone else on?'

Tehmeena was successfully diverted, and neither of them mentioned Kurt again.

As it turned out, the next few days were so busy, they had no time to chat at all. The arrival of fine spring weather brought an influx of customers, and besides her usual workload, Penny also had to pay several trips to Kurt's house in Richmond. The decorators were almost finished, and once the house was complete she'd be able to bring in the rest of the furnishings she'd chosen. But there was still one room that was just an empty shell — the master bedroom. The workmen were waiting for Penny's instructions, and for once, her imagination failed her. One day Kurt would be sharing this intimate space with the woman he married — whoever that level-headed person might turn out to be — and whenever Penny tried to picture his future wife, all her ideas faltered and dried up completely. As an experiment, she tried putting Cass in the scene, and at first, it worked quite well. She imagined the sort of room Cass might like — something eminently practical, with plenty of fitted wardrobes and maybe the odd country touch, like some white cotton curtains or floral cushions.

Penny closed her eyes, allowing her imagination to weave a slow picture. A few horsey prints appeared on the walls and a family photo on the bedside table. OK, this was good. But just as she was getting there, Kurt stepped into the imaginary bedroom and looked straight at her, his eyes grey and steady, the handsome half-smile on his lips that he reserved for her. Her vision shattered. No, no, no! She shut her eyes again, but it was no good. Everything had vanished. As soon as Kurt opened the door in her mind, there was room for nothing else.

After yet another call from the increasingly impatient decorators, she decided the only thing to do was phone Kurt himself and ask for help. She had resolved to have as little to do with him as possible, but the decorators were at a stand still, waiting for her decision. Since it seemed she was incapable of making one, there was no other option but to ask Kurt to step in.

His mobile rang only once before he picked it up. 'Hey, Penny. Everything OK?'

His deep voice had quickened with the familiar greeting. She'd forgotten how damn sexy he sounded. She closed her eyes. This was going to be even harder than she imagined.

'Penny?'

'Yes, I'm fine.' It was a lie, but at least her tongue had finally loosened.

'You heard from David?' There was a rough edge to his voice. 'Is he giving you trouble?'

'No, no it's nothing like that. There's no problem. I just need some advice. About your house.'

'Uhuh? Go ahead.'

There was no help for it. Taking a deep breath, Penny plunged in. 'The decorators have just about finished. There's just one room left to do before I can bring in all the furnishings.'

'Oh? What's left?'

'Your bedroom,' Penny blurted out. 'I

don't know what you want to do in there.'

There was a small pause. Then Kurt came back, the unmistakable hint of amusement flavouring his deep voice. 'You don't know what I want to do in my bedroom?'

'Yes. I mean no.' She stopped. It was a good job Kurt was on the other end of a phone. She'd been trying to stay cool and now this. This wasn't how the conversation was supposed to be going at all.

'Should I come over? I can show you what I want, if you like.'

Penny stood still. Kurt's voice had slowed, and his question hung quivering between them. There was a pause which seemed to go on and on, although it could only have been a couple of seconds. She heard him breathe in and then out again.

'Penny, if it were anyone else, I would be straight over on the back of that offer to show you exactly what I mean.' All of a sudden the smile had gone out of his voice. He carried on abruptly. 'How about I meet you there tomorrow? It will give me a chance to look over the rest of the house.'

If it were anyone else . . . Kurt's words gave her all the impetus she needed to keep her response business-like.

'Fine.' She was pleased with how cool her reply sounded, but when she pressed end on the call, she knew the conversation had been a disaster. The sound of Kurt's voice wiped her mind clean of any other thought than what he'd like to do in his bedroom. And now the effort it cost to keep wrenching her thoughts from a picture of Kurt undressing in an empty room took too much out of her. When she finally walked into his house the next day and trod the stairs to his bare, echoing bedroom, her mind was still full of delicious images . . . but none of them the sort she should be keeping in her head.

She stepped into the centre of the

room and took a long look around the stripped walls, the bare floorboards, and the grimy window, waiting for her mind to clear and for inspiration to come. Nothing.

The front door swung shut in the hallway beneath her, and Kurt's assured tread crossed the wooden floor and mounted the stairs. Then the bedroom door swung open, and he was there in the empty room.

Penny turned. For a moment, she was struck with a feeling of disorientation. She hadn't yet got used to the sight of Kurt in a suit and pictured him always in jeans and boots. He'd obviously just come from the office and was tugging his tie loose in a way that was causing her nerve endings to melt slowly with the heat of her thoughts.

Great, now she was thinking about watching him undress again. She turned her head, acknowledging Kurt's greeting brusquely before giving a quick sweep of her hand around the room.

'See? I've run out of ideas. Shall we

take a look around the rest of the house first? Maybe that might help.'

The warmth that lit Kurt's eyes on seeing her dimmed a little at her abruptness, but he gave his slow nod, holding the door wide for her to lead the way.

The house had changed dramatically since Kurt first brought her to it. The musty drabness was swept away, and the whole place breathed with renewed freshness and light. The hideous salmon bathroom had been ripped out and replaced with crisp white units. A smaller bathroom was fitted out in a similar style, and the bedrooms transformed with colours ranging from simple beige to dramatic red.

Penny led Kurt through the revamped space, anxiously awaiting his approval at the door of each room. When they finally reached the kitchen, her anxiety increased. She'd spent a great deal of time thinking about this room, wanting it to be perfect. She knew how important it was to Kurt to have a family, and the kitchen was the central gathering place. She retreated to the window to await his reaction, chewing her lip.

For a while, Kurt said nothing, gazing about him in silence, taking in the rich red of the floor tiles, the antique dresser and the family-sized, scrubbed table. When his eyes fell on the restored range, he did a double-take.

'Hey, you really managed to clean it up.' He stepped forward to where the range gleamed in magnificent glory in the old chimney-breast and bent to open one of the jet-black doors. 'No spiders.'

Penny gave him a happy grin. 'Nope. And it works, too. Although we fitted a real cooker as well, so you can use either.'

Kurt looked about, and Penny felt her anxiety gradually ebb away at his evident pleasure in everything he saw. When he moved over to the electric cooker and opened the door to look inside, some of her former liveliness returned. She tilted her head on one side.

'So,' she said. 'I suppose you'll be spending a lot of time in the kitchen? How are your cooking skills?'

He lifted his head and grinned back confidently. 'I'll have you know, people say I'm a great cook. Used to cook for my sister, Ann, every day until I left home. Her friends all said my steak is the best in Wyoming.'

Penny laughed. 'Wow! Do you know, I never really pictured you at home in the kitchen?'

'Guess you don't know that much about me.' Kurt was still smiling, but there was a hint of challenge in the way he spoke.

Instantly, Penny withdrew. Getting to know Kurt would mean revealing some of herself in return, and she had no intention of even so much as hinting at how deep her feelings for him ran. Of putting her heart out in the open and being treated like a kid sister with a crush. Kurt straightened up, the smile leaving his face.

'So, have we done here?' he said coolly. 'Shall we take a look at the bedroom?'

Penny nodded, her expression taut. Although the feeling of constraint between them almost brought her to tears, she needed to get this over with. She turned back to the hallway and headed up the stairs. In the bedroom, the late afternoon sun was spreading some warmth across the bare floorboards, and the dust swirled a little as Penny opened the door. She made a beeline for the window and opened it. The air outside was warm and still. Kurt stepped across the room and stood beside her, his eyes scanning the bare walls.

'You've done such a great job in the rest of the house. Everything's perfect.'

She turned her head, her expression brightening a little. At least she'd got something right.

'It's been great,' she said. 'I've

enjoyed it. The decorators were great guys, and the house is a dream. It was a pleasure doing everything.'

'Then why stop here?' He gestured to the empty room. 'I don't understand. You had such a vision for the rest of the house. Why draw a blank in this room?'

Penny followed the arc his arm had made. The bare room gave no answer, and his words echoed in the dusty air. She frowned at the plaster walls.

'I don't know. That's why I thought it would be better to ask you to come over.' She looked up at him then. 'What you said in the kitchen was right. I don't really know you. I don't really understand your plans for the future. I can't picture the sort of wife you're looking for, and I still don't really understand your motives for marrying if you're not marrying for love.'

Kurt had turned with her and was facing into the room. The warm light from the window fell on his face, and his long lashes swept downward as he studied the floor. He put his hands in the pockets of his suit trousers and leaned back on the window sill.

When he didn't answer straightaway, Penny continued. 'I feel I need to know, or I can't finish the room. Does that seem odd?'

He threw her a brief, warm smile then. 'No, it doesn't seem odd to me. I understand you. It's important for you to feel something . . . ' He left off whatever he'd been about to say to let his gaze travel around the room. 'You've given so much feeling to everything you've done in this house. Everything you do, you take on with a passion. It's what I — ' He broke off abruptly, leaving the unfinished sentence hanging unspoken in the silence.

Penny stared at him. *It's what I . . . ?* What had he been about to say? But Kurt's head was bent, his features hidden, and he remained silent for such a long time, Penny could almost believe he'd forgotten she was there.

A muscle trembled in his clenched jaw, but when he finally spoke his slow voice sounded even more collected than usual. 'Ever since I left home I wanted a family,' he said. 'I wanted two kids, a girl and a boy, and all I wanted was to give them a happy home. The sort of home me and Ann never got.' He laughed without humour. 'That's been my dream. And now I have the financial security and the house, so all I need is a wife and children.'

Penny drew in a breath to reply, but Kurt turned to her before she could speak. 'I know what you're thinking. That I'm looking at things backward. First should come the falling in love and all the romantic drama, then marriage, then the kids are an after-thought.' His voice had roughened. 'But that's not what I want for my kids. I told you before, passion is short-lived. I'm looking for a woman who shares the same values, who's not looking for any romance and who can provide a stable home. The sort of home me and Ann never had.'

There was a roughness in his voice

that Penny had never heard in him before. She stole a glance at his profile. His head was bent, the expression masked behind hooded eyelids, making him seem remote despite their physical proximity. Penny was tempted to reach out for him, to touch his hand at least, but his hands were rammed in his pockets, and in any case, the moment was soon gone.

He straightened up to give another quick scan round the bare room. 'I appreciate everything you're doing,' he said. 'Since you've asked my opinion, I'd say how about using some neutral colours in here? Something that doesn't draw the eye too much.'

Penny stared at him, her mouth opening uselessly. Eventually, she pulled herself away from the window. 'Neutral colours,' she repeated expressionlessly. 'Fine. I just need to be in here alone for a few minutes. Just to have a look around again and to think.'

'Sure.' Kurt pulled himself upright. For a couple of seconds, there was a taut silence. Then he turned, his tread sounding hollowly on the bare floor as he headed for the stairway.

Once alone, Penny moved to gaze out of the window, shivering a little. The air had grown colder as the afternoon progressed. She reached out a hand to pull shut the pane. Outside the sun was sinking over the park, and the shadows cast by the trees were lengthening over the grasslands. Penny pressed her forehead against the cool glass.

She had been right in her intuition. She was unable to visualise Kurt's bedroom because he himself had no idea what it was to have an intimate relationship. *Neutral colours*. Even his chosen colour scheme said everything. Penny was unbearably saddened. She pitied the woman Kurt eventually married and even pitied his future children. He meant the best for them, but nothing could be controlled in the way Kurt thought it could. A home could be stable, but it would also be sterile without a deeply loving relationship at its core. She hoped with all the strength in her gentle heart that one day Kurt would find the woman who could teach him this, and that he wouldn't throw away any chance he had at happiness.

Out in the park, the last rays of the sun caught the surface of the pond, causing it to shimmer grey and blue in the spring breeze. *I don't like to feel boxed in*. She remembered Kurt's words to her on their first walk outdoors, his homesickness for the great spaces and the sky over Wyoming, and as she turned to look at the empty bedroom the germ of an idea began spreading slow roots. Maybe that was the answer. Maybe she should use this room to show Kurt that passionate love wasn't a prison to box you in. Passionate love was nothing to fear. On the contrary, it could be a liberation.

She moved away from the window, taking a few steps around the perimeter and casting her eyes over the walls. Yes, she thought, and in that moment, all her indecision was swept away in a sudden feeling of recklessness. She would forget Kurt's neutral colours, forget his neutral dating plans, and forget his neutral images of marriage. She refused to make this room a prison for an empty relationship. She would open up her imagination and make Kurt's bedroom a final, passionate gift from herself — and risk everything.

Kurt reached his apartment that evening suffering from an intense lassitude, such as he'd rarely before experienced. All his plans for the future seemed grey and dull as London fog. When he'd first decided on buying the house, he'd had a real sense of purpose. It was one more step on the ladder of success: a good career, a good income, a good house, a good wife, and a good family. Fifteen years ago, when he left college, it hadn't seemed too much to ask. Now it seemed he might as well be asking for the moon. What the hell had happened to his carefully laid plans in recent weeks?

He threw the jacket of his suit onto a counter and switched on the kitchen light. A fluorescent glare lit up the white space, hurting his eyes. He pulled out a bottle of bourbon, poured a decent slug into a glass, and leaned back against the units, taking in the gleaming stainless steel, the black worktops bare of any sign of habitation. He hadn't realised how soulless this room was until he walked into the kitchen Penny furnished for him. She'd transformed that room — just like she had the rest of the house — into somewhere warm, welcoming, full of her personality. A home.

It's what I love about you. Those were the words Kurt had left unsaid that afternoon, alone with her in his empty bedroom. He felt all the hopelessness of the unfinished sentence like a terrifying weight on his chest.

Out of nowhere Alex's perspiring face that night in the bar came into his mind and his drunken words, *Dude, that girl's really something, isn't she?* In the bright light of his kitchen, Kurt's fingers gripped the glass. Alex, with his vast experience of women, had realised in the space of a single evening what it had taken Kurt weeks to understand. Penny was really something.

In a few weeks' time, once his house was finished, he would have no more reason to see her. They could keep in touch as friends, but he also knew that avenue would be a dead end. She would keep backing off until they lost touch altogether. He remembered his offer to give her riding lessons and the way her face had shuttered. Her polite evasion had told him everything. She wasn't interested.

It wasn't like him to feel so uncertain. He had made a decision to put his dating on hold until the house was ready. He hadn't really analysed why, but now he finally acknowledged the real reason, that being around Penny so much messed with his head. Each time he'd dated another woman recently, he could only think about how much more fun it would have been if he'd been with Penny. No one else seemed to fill his senses as she did, so that all he could think of was reaching for her and holding her close, holding her until her soft, expressive body was his and all she was became a very part of him. When he thought of her, every atom of her being filled his senses, and her very essence seemed to leap through his veins.

He closed his eyes. What the hell was he going to do? The perfectly suitable women he'd dated were just pallid shadows in comparison, and yet he'd been counting on finding a wife this way. He opened his eyes to stare into his half-drained glass. Once he wasn't seeing Penny so much, maybe life would return to its previous steady normality, and he could put his plans for the future back into action. He threw down the remaining contents of the glass in one last mouthful. He was a strong man. Surely he could find the strength within him to forget Penny and get his life back on track.

It was just that when he thought of a life without her, somehow the future seemed to stretch into infinity, dull as ditchwater.

★   ★   ★

It was fortunate for Penny that for the next few days she had little opportunity to let her mind dwell on Kurt. Work was busy. Occasionally she would allow her thoughts to wander, and she would recall the time Kurt had brought her the tulips and he had kissed her cheek. She found it hard not to dwell on this memory, reliving the warmth of his kiss. She would find herself replaying the scene in her head, each time having it end with his lips on hers. When she was at work, it was easy to bring herself back to reality. The scene would finish there in her mind, and she could force herself back to her surroundings. At home in the silence of her bedroom, it was a different story. A different scene altogether. The kiss was just the beginning of a fantasy which was full of such erotic longing Penny would find herself burning and sleepless, rising the next day sure she could never meet Kurt's eyes in real life ever again.

It was lucky they would only need to meet a handful more times before the house was finished. Maybe even just one more meeting. She could show him the final stage and leave it at that. The thought should have made her happy, but instead, she was appearing at work looking increasingly tired and drained.

'Hey, did you see the local news last night?' Tehmeena called to her excitedly one morning. Penny had barely opened the shop door. The fine spring had been short-lived, and she was removing her wet coat and trying to shake her umbrella without splashing too much water around.

'No,' she called back a little grumpily, throwing her coat over a hook. 'Granddad wanted to watch golf all evening.'

'Shame. It was on at six. Why don't you catch up on the internet now? I doubt we'll get many customers this morning. Not in this downpour.'

'Catch up with what? What's good in the local area — more shoplifting and arson?' Penny dumped her bag down beside her desk and switched on her laptop. It wasn't like her to be crotchety, but the past few days, she'd been far from her usual cheerful self.

Tehmeena pursed her lips. 'It's not all doom and gloom around here, you know.' She turned back to the open china cabinet, which she'd been in the process of dusting. 'Take a look on the net and see for yourself,' she called over her shoulder. 'Some people perform acts of charity.'

Penny logged onto the news channel without much enthusiasm, flicking through for the previous evening's local report. She found the relevant item, clicked play, and immediately the usual impossibly coiffed newsreader came into view. For ten minutes, Penny listened to her talk about how teenagers had burned a whole warehouse down, her teeth showing in a relentlessly cheerful smile the whole time. There followed an intense debate around the news table as members of the local community discussed opportunities for teenagers in the area and how to combat the rise of mindless crime.

Penny was just about to call over to Tehmeena that actually it was all doom and gloom, when the newsreader turned to the camera. 'Well, if you think the rise in teenage crime heralds an era of doom and gloom, think again. An American finance worker is sponsoring a scheme to bring something different to the kids in the inner city. Take a look at this.'

Penny's jaw dropped. The screen filled with a shot of Richmond Park, the camera panning slowly past trees coming into leaf and deer in the distance, before coming to rest on a group of horses trotting across the grasslands. In the middle of the group, and looking magnificent astride a gigantic white horse, was the unmistakable figure of Kurt. Even from a distance and with a smart riding helmet covering his dark blond head, Penny would have known him anywhere. She leaned forward and stared at the screen, open-mouthed.

The shot of trotting horses was cut away to be replaced by a group of teenagers dismounting awkwardly in a stable yard. Penny wasn't surprised to see Cass was also one of the riders. The woman dismounted in a swift, stylish movement, giving the camera a glamorous smile before turning away to help one of the kids. Over the scene, the newsreader described how Kurt, together with the stables in Richmond, had put together a programme to help disadvantaged city children by offering riding lessons and introducing them to the abundant wildlife in the park. Next thing, Kurt's head filled the screen, and he was giving that slow, courteous nod. He appeared to be looking right into

Penny's eyes, and her heart turned over with a thump.

'I'm lucky to have this wonderful park on my doorstep, and I wanted to share my good fortune with kids who don't get the same sense of space. Being boxed in is bad for the spirit.'

The camera panned back to reveal Cass standing by his side, looking up at him adoringly. They made a striking couple. The interviewer asked a few more questions, which Cass and Kurt took turns in answering, and then the film finished to cut back to the studio.

Penny sank back in her chair. So this was the charitable project Kurt had been working on. How like him to carry out his plans in such a quiet way. He was quiet and reserved and would never dream of bragging. He would never dream of bigging himself up about anything. Just like when they first met and she'd thought he was a simple cowboy when all along he was head of a massive company.

She rubbed her fingers across her

forehead. Kurt also hadn't mentioned just how involved he was with Cass. Maybe because their relationship just wasn't that important . . . or maybe because he was hoping they'd become much closer. She reached forward and closed the lid of her laptop with a sigh. Whatever, it was none of her business. And if he didn't date Cass, he'd only be dating someone else anyway, so there was no point thinking about it.

She looked up to find several customers had entered the shop whilst she'd been engrossed in the news. She stood up quickly, but before taking up her position behind the counter, she went over to where Tehmeena was relocking the china cabinet.

'Thanks for telling me,' she said. 'It was great to see. And you're right — it's not all doom and gloom.'

Although if it wasn't all doom and gloom, why did she feel so utterly miserable?

9

Penny perched on a stool in Kurt's bedroom and lifted the final painting to the wall, arching her back precariously to check everything was straight. She'd given the decorators their instructions, and the room was finally painted. She was now alone, putting in the last touches. The furniture and furnishings in the rest of the rooms were complete, and the whole house breathed with new life. For once Penny allowed herself a glow of satisfaction. Kurt was sure to be happy.

Happy with everything — except maybe this room. She stepped down from the chair and stood back, casting a doubtful glance around the set of paintings. What if she were wrong? What if everything she'd done in here was totally over the top and he hated it? She chewed her lip in a state of anxiety.

He'd asked for something neutral, for goodness' sake, not this explosion of passion. She twisted her head to examine the paintings again before giving a resigned shrug. It was too late, anyway. If Kurt didn't like it, he could always rip out the whole bedroom after she'd gone and paint it magnolia. She would never know, in any case, because once she'd given back her set of keys, they would no longer be in contact.

She took a last fatalistic look round and was just putting on her jacket to leave when her mobile rang, making her jump in the quiet of the house.

'Hey,' Kurt said.

'Hey. I saw you on television. What a surprise. Nice work. You looked good.' *You looked good*. Penny rolled her eyes at herself.

'Thanks. Although to be honest, Cass did most of the work. I just showed up and rode a horse.'

Penny laughed as she shrugged on her jacket. 'According to the news, you did a good job persuading the stables to work with you, and you raised all the money. That can't have been easy.'

'Yeah, I guess the finance side hasn't been easy. Actually, that's why I'm calling. Or partly.'

'Oh?'

'Thing is, Cass organised a charity auction to try and raise money.'

'Oh,' Penny said again. 'Are you looking for donations?' She began a rapid mental review of suitable items from the shop's stock, which Kurt interrupted quickly.

'Yeah, a donation would be great. But actually, it's not that, it's something else. Thing is, the event is a ball as well as an auction.'

There was a short pause. It was unlike Kurt not to come to the point directly. Penny sensed the hesitation in his voice and waited. He drew in a breath and the rest of his words came out in an uncharacteristic rush.

'I was wondering if you'd come with me?'

She almost gasped aloud. 'Me? I

mean, what about Cass?'

'Well, that's the thing. Cass and I were supposed to go together, but she's ill. Of course Cass being involved in the project, and all, it made sense for us to go together. But now she can't make it.'

'I see.' Penny halted. So, she was second choice. She understood Kurt's embarrassment, asking her to fill in like this, but nobody liked feeling second-best. She tried not to let a wave of disappointment wash over her.

Kurt broke the uncomfortable silence. 'I understand how this seems, asking you at the last minute and all, but I'd love it if you said yes.' His urging was laced with uncharacteristic uncertainty. 'I'd rather go with you than anyone else.'

There was a silence. Penny took in a breath, but before she could answer, Kurt added, 'And it's for charity.'

She gave a short, defeated laugh. 'Oh well, if you put it like that. Where and when? And most important, what do I wear?'

Penny could almost hear him leap up with relief. 'Seven p.m. next Saturday, Park Lane,' he said, an injection of cheerfulness in his voice. 'You got a ball gown?'

'More than most people ever dream of,' she said drily, thinking of her mother's collection. 'I'll look one out.'

'It's great you're willing to do this for me.' His voice dropped. 'Now I'm looking forward to it.'

'No problem.' Penny was proud of the cool way she handled his request. She was especially proud of remaining cool in a bedroom that was the absolute opposite of cool. It was hard to look at the décor and not feel her skin burn. The whole room radiated heat.

'And Kurt?' she added tentatively. 'Your house is just about ready. Maybe you could come over on Sunday? After the ball?'

'Sure. Can't wait. Thanks, Penny, you're awesome, kid.'

Penny ended the call and stuffed her phone in her jacket pocket. *Awesome, kid*. Fabulous. The kid sister, wheeled in in second place behind the glamorous girlfriend. She put her hand on the door handle and turned to take a final look around the bedroom. After Kurt moved in, it would be the last she'd ever see of it. She stepped over to straighten the painting on the wall one last time before leaving the room, pulling the door shut behind her.

★　★　★

Choosing something to wear for her regular night out with the girls often caused Penny a headache. She would go through her entire wardrobe, flinging clothes on the bed at random, only to discover she had absolutely nothing to wear. For most people, trying to find an evening dress for an exclusive ball at one of London's top hotels would present an even greater problem, but not for Penny. She went straight to the trunk which had belonged to her mother and opened the lid. Everything inside was neatly packed away in tissue paper — literally dozens of dresses which her mother had worn on red carpets around the world. Penny's grandmother had refused to dispose of the ball gowns, insisting that when Penny grew up she would want to wear them herself. By the time Penny was a teenager, however, it was perfectly obvious she was never going to step into her mother's glamorous shoes and become another Megan Rose. Her grandmother had struggled for the rest of her life to conceal her disappointment.

Penny knelt down and lifted the top layer of tissue paper from the trunk. A couple of loose sequins slid to the floor. She picked them up, feeling the metal, cold and hard, in her palm, and for a minute or two, she froze on her knees, staring down into the trunk.

What, she asked herself, do you think you are doing, going to this ball, all glammed up? A ridiculous Cinderella. The dripping well of misery within her finally overflowed. A tread on the landing warned her when her granddad entered the room. Too overcome to turn, she bent her head over the trunk. Her grandfather paused in the doorway and then took a few slow steps across the room. She heard him crouch awkwardly beside her, and then he took her hand in his.

Instantly, a sob burst from her. 'Granddad, I'm sick of feeling second-best.' She knew she sounded self-pitying, but despair overwhelmed her, and she was past caring. The words caught painfully in her throat. 'I've tried and tried to feel beautiful and glamorous like Mum, but everything in my life is always grey and miserable.'

Her grandfather reached over without speaking and pulled her to him. The rub of his sweater was comforting beneath her wet cheeks. Her shoulders heaved once or twice as he patted her awkwardly. After a while, he cleared his throat, the frail hands tightening their grip.

'Penny, listen to me,' he said, a catch in his voice. 'Everyone loved your mother; it's true. But they loved a mirage. She was a dream, an image on screen. The only people who really loved her — and I mean truly loved the person she was, faults and all — were your dad and your grandmother. And me. Your mother wasn't perfect. If you'd had a chance to get to know her, you'd realise that.' He pushed his granddaughter gently away and pulled a handkerchief out of his pocket, pressing it into her hand. 'Here, take this.'

She blew her nose noisily. When she'd composed herself a little, he sank back stiffly on his heels and took hold of her hand. 'I've told you before, Penny. You're not second-best. You're not second-best to me, and one day you'll find the man who makes you feel loved the way you should be.'

Penny squeezed his hand but didn't meet his eyes. 'Maybe.' She lifted the handkerchief to her nose and blew again.

'Definitely.'

Penny heard the smile in her grandfather's voice and looked up. His pale blue eyes were slightly damp, but there was a definite twinkle in them. 'I'd say before too long you'll definitely find there's a man out there who loves you for who you are. Sooner maybe than you think.' He squeezed her hand again, a grave smile on his lips. 'But promise one thing. Don't ever accept second-best. You're worth more than that.'

Penny reached up and kissed his cheek. 'Well at least you believe in me, Granddad.'

'I do.' He gave her another brief hug. 'But you have to believe in yourself,' he finished gravely.

Her grandfather's words were a comfort but did little to dent Penny's deep-rooted unhappiness. The secret to alleviating her depression, she told herself for the hundredth time, was to have nothing more to do with Kurt. The constant necessity of hiding her feelings for him was wearing her out.

She lifted out the first of her mother's evening dresses and let the cool fabric slip through her fingers. The dresses were crying out to be worn. And attending the ball with Kurt would be the last evening she'd ever spend with him, so then what the heck? She might as well summon up all her reserves and go out dressed to kill.

* * *

Kurt stepped out of the taxi and walked up the short drive to Penny's front door. He had been ridiculously happy when she agreed to come with him, but now as he stood in front of her house, he was surprised to find his heart rattling along at an uncomfortable rate. He lifted the knocker and gave it a short, hard rap before standing back, straightening his bowtie with one hand and adjusting the bouquet he was holding in the other. The door opened wide. Penny greeted him with a cool smile which altered dramatically as soon as her eyes fell on the bouquet.

'Roses.' Her eyes widened in wonder.

Kurt said nothing. He found himself staring at Penny in the same dumbstruck fashion he had greeted her that night outside the restaurant. If she'd looked like a princess on that occasion, tonight she was a queen. Her hair was swept up, revealing naked shoulders that rose out of an elegant black evening dress. A diamond chain glittered around her neck. The hands she extended to receive the bouquet were clad in long black evening gloves which climbed the length of her graceful arms. Kurt could barely tear his eyes away from the creaminess of her naked skin. The thought of peeling off those gloves was almost as erotic as asking her to step out of the dress.

Heat suffused his neck and travelled upwards to his cheekbones, and the beat of his heart swelled to a crescendo in his ears. It was lucky for him that

Penny was entirely absorbed in the bouquet.

'You brought roses.' She gazed in wonder at the white blooms before raising them to her face to take in the fragrance.

'Yes.' Kurt's voice was a little hoarse. He cleared his throat. 'I thought you'd like them.'

'I do.' Her bright eyes lifted and caught his in such a beam of wondrous delight he almost fell backwards.

'You did something to your hair,' he blurted and then cursed inwardly. She looked awesome. Was that all he could find to say? That smooth-talking Alex would have been sure to have the right words on his tongue.

Penny lifted a hand to the loose tendrils skimming her bare neck. 'I had it done at the salon. Do you like it?'

Like it? He was resisting the urge to pull out all the pins that were holding it up and plunge his hands into it.

He nodded, his mouth dry. 'You look good.'

Her cheeks went a faint pink. 'You look good, too,' she said, dropping her eyes. 'I'll just give this bouquet to Granddad to look after.'

She disappeared into the house, and he heard her murmur a few words to her grandfather. The next minute she reappeared, a silver scarf around her shoulders.

'Granddad says hello. He can't come to the door because he's in the middle of fixing a two-hundred-year-old watch.'

Kurt gave her his arm and smiled down at her. 'It would be terrible to disturb him.'

'Oh, he's happy as the proverbial pig.' Her eyes twinkled. 'Now he can spread oil and bits of watch all over the kitchen table.'

Their easy chatter set the tone for the conversation for the rest of the evening: lightly humorous, saying nothing important, and above all, revealing nothing of the deep current of their emotions. When Penny walked into the ballroom

on Kurt's arm and saw how enchant-
ingly it had been decorated, she gave
his arm a playful squeeze and looked up
at him, her eyes teasing.

'Did you choose the colour scheme?'

He looked down, laughing. 'Caught
out. No, it was Cass. She's done a great
job organising even though she's had to
work from her sick bed.'

'Really?' Penny widened her eyes in
concern. 'I had no idea. Shouldn't she
be resting?'

Kurt grinned. 'Oh, don't worry, she's
well enough to pick up the phone.' He
bent his head to her ear. 'I'll tell you a
secret, but she'd be mad if you told
anyone else. She's got chickenpox.'

'O-o-h.' Penny's mouth rounded. Her
expression was still full of concern
— after all, chickenpox was no joke for
adults — but she was reassured on
catching Kurt's eye to find he was still
smiling.

'She's fine,' he insisted. 'She's just
not allowed out of the house until the
spots have gone. She's annoyed and

tired more than anything. And upset at missing a party. She's like a spoiled kid,' he added as an afterthought.

Penny glanced up at him. It wasn't a very lover-like statement. 'Well it's a shame,' she said. She did feel genuinely sorry for Cass. But there was no time to discuss it further, because Kurt was spotted by some of the riders from the stables, and they were soon surrounded by a chattering group of people. After the introductions, and when it became obvious that the conversation would revolve solely around horses, Penny took the opportunity of slipping away to look through the objects up for auction.

There was a sizeable display on the auction table. As was to be expected, most of the donations had an equestrian theme. There were free riding lessons at the stables and a photograph signed by an Olympic show-jumper. Penny had donated a vintage brooch, fashioned in the shape of a horse. But for those people attending who didn't live and breathe horses there were a few other items, and Penny found herself drawn to a diamond bracelet, donated by a local jeweller's. She lifted it out of its silk-lined box and held it carefully in one hand to examine it. It was beautifully fashioned so that the diamonds twisted round each other like slim ribbons. She couldn't resist trying it on over her long black gloves, and was just holding her wrist out to admire it when she heard a familiar voice in her ear.

'Mmmm. Looking good.'

She started guiltily and whirled round to find Alex's lively brown eyes on hers. 'Alex! I had no idea you were coming.'

Alex's was the first familiar face she had encountered, and she couldn't prevent a wide smile lighting her face. He grinned back, running his eyes all the way from her chic hairstyle to the tips of her silver heels before giving an admiring whistle.

'It's good to see you, too.' He lifted his eyes to hers. 'Kurt's a lucky guy.'

Penny felt herself redden. 'Oh, Kurt and I — ' she said. 'We've just come as friends, that's all.'

She lifted her arm to try and pull off the bracelet, but it had become stuck on one of the buttons of her gloves.

'Here, let me.' Alex bent his head and caught hold of her wrist. 'Just friends, huh?' He looked up at her, suddenly serious. 'Then Kurt's an idiot.'

He released the bracelet from her wrist with one deft movement. Penny looked into his face without speaking. Alex's words should have been taken as a light-hearted compliment, but instead, she felt all the misery of the past few weeks descend on her. She glanced over her shoulder. Kurt had taken his seat at their table, and his head was bent attentively towards one of the guests. As though he felt her eyes on him, he looked up and gave her a warm smile before turning back to his neighbour. It was a friendly gesture, but it did little to lift the chill that descended on her.

She turned back to Alex and forced a

smile. 'Good to see you again.'

'Sure. I'll catch you later. Save me a dance, huh?' He fixed her with a sympathetic look before dropping a wink with his old mix of mischievous flirtation. Penny gave him a grin and went to join Kurt at their table. He stood as she approached, bending over her with his usual heart-stopping courtesy to pull out her chair.

'I see Alex is up to his old tricks,' he murmured in her ear as she took her seat. He sat down next to her and bent his head, so no-one else could hear. 'Just make sure you don't get drunk again.'

Penny's mouth flew open. She twisted her head to find Kurt's grey eyes laughing down at her.

'I wasn't drunk,' she protested in a mock whisper. 'How many more times?'

'Sure.' He patted her hand with a grin. 'Just lay off the liquor.'

She kicked him under the table and was gratified to see him wince.

If Penny had wanted her last evening

with Kurt to be light-hearted fun, then her wish was granted. The other guests at her table were friendly and lively — a mixture of Kurt's acquaintances from the stables and staff from a charity for disadvantaged children. It was a novelty for Penny to be away from the world of antiques for once, and she was quite content to sit back and listen to them chatter. As the waiters were clearing the last of their plates, the head of the stables — a small, wiry man with a smile that split his face — leaned across the table.

'I expect you'll know all about auctions in your trade, Penny.'

'Yes, and I love them. It's such an exciting atmosphere and such a great feeling when you win on a bargain.'

One of the charity workers leaned over. 'Seen anything that takes your fancy tonight?'

'Yes.' Her eyes lit up. 'There's a gorgeous diamond bracelet. But I expect the bidding will go way out of my league on that, though.' She pulled

266

a face. 'Not to worry. And there's a signed golf programme I'm bidding on for my grandfather.'

Later, Kurt put his hand on her arm, and she turned her head. His face was close to hers, a serious question in his eyes. 'If you want that bracelet so much, I'll bid on it,' he said.

'No.' Penny recoiled in horror. 'It will be far too much. And it wasn't a hint. I forbid you to bid for it.'

Kurt said nothing, but a small smile formed on his lips. Knowing how stubborn he could be once he'd made up his mind, she caught hold of his arm. 'Don't bid for it, Kurt,' she begged earnestly. 'Promise.'

The smile widened on Kurt's lips. He took her hand in his and examined it, pretending to deliberate, whilst Penny waited anxiously.

'OK,' he said, releasing her fingers with a defeated sigh. 'If it means so much to you, I promise I won't bid on it.'

Penny stared at him suspiciously. He

had capitulated far too easily. But there was no time for further questions, because just then, someone came and tapped Kurt's shoulder. It was time for him to get up and make his speech.

The chattering at the tables fell to a hush. Penny gazed round the room as Kurt made his way to the mic. She'd never seen him in action in public before. Without seeming to make an effort, he had a physical presence and the knack of focusing attention. From the moment he stood, even before he reached the podium, people quieted to listen to what he had to say. He spoke seriously about the charity's aims, keeping his comments brief and to the point. He told the audience they shouldn't waste time listening to him when they could be dipping their hands in their pockets. His speech finished on a humorously revealing note.

'I was a tough kid growing up, looking for trouble, and if I'd grown up in a city with other tough kids, I can tell you, I'd be in jail right now. Kids need freedom. That's why I want to thank you for your support. Happy bidding.'

The guests laughed, and when Kurt stood back from the microphone, a ragged cheer went up around the room. Penny heard Alex's voice amongst the others as she put her hands together and experienced a swell of pride. Kurt made his way through the tables of guests, stopping now and then to greet acquaintances. He bent over to say a few words to Alex at the next table, and she watched in surprise as Alex looked in her direction before giving him a grin and a thumbs up. Then Kurt was back beside her. She greeted him with a wide smile as he retook his seat.

'That was a great speech,' she said. 'It's a shame Cass couldn't be here to share the thanks.'

He lifted his glass to her. 'Thanks,' he said. 'And thanks for coming with me tonight. It means a lot.'

'It's a great cause. And it's been fun.' Penny raised her glass. She meant what she said, it had been surprisingly fun, and she was determined not to think about the next day or their final meeting. If this was all the time she had left, then she might as well live in the moment. She lifted her glass to her lips. When she replaced it on the table, Kurt took her hand in his. To her surprise, he twined his fingers around hers and slid their joined hands downwards to rest together on his broad knee. The wool of his trousers rubbed against her fingers. The small gesture was unexpected, and it sent the blood rushing to her heart, enveloping her in a sudden faintness. His gaze caught hers directly, steadily. His neighbour spoke, and he turned away, leaving her hand caught in his, his fingers wrapped around hers in a warm clasp.

The heat of Kurt's thigh beneath her fingers, the scratch of the woollen fabric on the soft flesh of her hand and the weight of his strong hand were enough to fill her senses to the exclusion of all else. She could barely concentrate, and so it was several minutes before she registered above the hum in her ears that the auction had actually begun. All around the room, hands were flying up in the air. The auctioneer had launched into his swift banter, and items were moving rapidly under his hammer.

Fortunately, Penny realised just in time that the signed golf programme was next. Her free hand shot up in competition with one of Kurt's colleagues on the other side of the room. The price mounted steadily, but Penny was determined. She knew she was paying over the odds, but the money was for a good cause, and in any case, she wanted to repay her grandfather for all his words of kindness in the previous few days.

Eventually Kurt's colleague realised he was bidding against someone more determined than he, and with some loud banter from the rest of his table, he dropped his hand in laughing defeat, declining to bid any further.

The auctioneer looked over in Penny's direction and swung down his hammer. 'Sold to the woman in black.'

'Yes,' she cried, eyes sparkling with pleasure. Kurt smiled at her childlike delight, and his fingers tightened on hers under the table.

Several more items followed, including the vintage brooch Penny donated, which fetched far more than it was worth. And then the diamond bracelet was on the block. Penny raised her eyes to Kurt. She gripped his hand warningly.

'Sure you don't want to change your mind?' he asked. 'I'm happy to buy it for you. This is your last chance.'

'No. Remember your promise,' she said in a low voice.

'All right.' He shrugged, laughing down at her. 'You know you'll be sorry when someone else buys it.'

Immediately, as if on cue, Alex's hand shot into the air. Kurt turned to her. 'What did I tell you? Now you've definitely lost your chance. Buying it for one of his girlfriends, I'll bet.'

'He might not be,' Penny answered,

widening her eyes in innocence. 'He could be buying it for his mum. Let's not be judgmental.'

'Buying it for his mum,' Kurt repeated, teasing her on her English pronunciation. He looked over at Alex's handsome, determined face and laughed out loud at the thought.

The price rose steadily. Alex was in competition with at least two others, including the head of the stables, but still his hand waved and waved again. At one stage, as the price climbed well beyond what the bracelet was worth, Penny thought she saw him throw an uncertain glance in their direction. The head of the stables dropped his hand and gave a defeated laugh. Kurt leaned back in his chair, his face impassive. Eventually the hammer went down on what Penny thought an exorbitant price. Alex sat back, a relieved smile on his face, accepting the congratulations around the table.

Kurt leaned over to her. 'I'm sure that'll make his mum very happy,' he whispered. Penny pinched his fingers under the table, not deigning to answer.

By the time the lights dimmed and the jazz band started tuning up, a feeling of weariness was beginning to creep over Penny. She'd been determined to enjoy the evening as much as possible, but the previous miserable sleepless nights were beginning to take their toll. When Kurt asked her to dance, she stood and almost swayed into his arms.

'Hey, you OK?' He looked down at her, concern etched on his face. 'You look pale. Has it been a long evening?'

'Yes, but it's been a good evening.' She lifted her face to his with a small smile. 'I don't want to go home yet.'

He regarded her steadily for a moment and then gave the slow nod that never failed to send her heart pounding.

'All right then, just one dance. After that, I'll take you home.'

His hand was warm on the small of her back as he guided her to the dance floor, and then his arms enfolded her, his hands travelling gently the length of her naked back. The heat of his skin penetrated the fabric of his shirt, and she pressed her cheek close to the warmth of him, her weariness swept away by a thrilling lassitude. His chest rose in a sudden deep breath, and the strong beat of his heart thudded under her cheek. When she tilted her face up to his, she found him gazing down at her, eyes dark. She arched back, and his hands tightened on her bare skin. Her lips parted, and she watched his eyes drift down to her mouth. He drew in another breath, and then bent his head to her ear, his mouth grazing her soft flesh.

'Come, it's time to go.' His breath was warm on the tender skin beneath her ear. He loosened his arms from around her and turned her gently. 'Fetch your things and wait for me in the hotel lobby.'

10

In the draught from the rotating doors in reception, Penny shivered in her thin wrap.

'Here.' Kurt strode towards her, pulling off his jacket. 'Why didn't you bring a warmer wrap?' He brought the suit coat around her, letting his hands rest on her shoulders. 'You're shivering.'

Her shoulders stiffened a little under his fingers. When she spoke, her voice was cool. 'I'm not your kid sister.'

Kurt stared in astonishment at her averted head. 'I'm sorry. I saw you shivering and was worried you were getting cold.'

Her stiff body softened a little under his hands. She pulled his jacket around her, burying herself in its warmth. Her face was pale, a little withdrawn, but she looked up and gave him a small smile. 'Thanks for the jacket.'

A beam of yellow headlights caught the revolving door, and she picked up her clutch from the desk to make for the waiting taxi. Outside the hotel, with no jacket to protect him, the cold night air penetrated Kurt's shirt sleeves, causing the hairs to stand on his skin. The warmth between him and Penny evaporated into the night, and his heart began to sink. For a few tantalising moments this evening he had felt her reserve melt, but now the barriers she had built around herself seemed to have dropped firmly back into place. He slid into the cold seat beside her, and she shifted surreptitiously away from him. His heart sank further. The distance she made between them wasn't enough to be obvious, but there it was. The physical barrier was in place.

She turned her head towards him. 'Thanks for a lovely evening.' There was a small smile on her lips, and for an instant, her features resumed their openness.

He nodded his head slowly and saw

her eyes gleam in response. For a moment, they gazed at each other without speaking. The dull light from the streetlamps played over her, and her eyes were wide and luminous in the dark.

'I got you a present,' he said and watched her dark brows rise in surprise. 'Put your hand in my jacket pocket.'

She reached a hand down and fumbled through his jacket and then, with a small gasp, drew out a jewellery box. She flipped open the lid, and the diamond bracelet glittered dully in the orange light filtering through the cab. She turned to him, her lips parted in astonishment.

'How did you do this? Did you buy it from Alex?'

'No.' Kurt couldn't prevent a grin spreading across his face at her wide-eyed astonishment. 'You made me promise not to bid on it, so I didn't. I asked Alex to bid on my behalf.'

'Oh,' she cried. 'That's cheating. I can't believe you did that.' She looked down at the bracelet. 'It's beautiful. No one's ever bought me anything like it.' When she turned her face to his, her eyes were shimmering. 'I feel as though I should give it back. It's not right.'

'Give it back?' He took her hand in his, as he had at the ball, and brought it to rest on his knee. 'Now what would I do with it?' He smiled, pleased he had been able to give her so much pleasure. Her fingers tightened in his, and she dropped her eyes, pretending to examine the bracelet, but he sensed something was wrong. He increased the pressure on her hand unconsciously.

'Why would it not be right?' he asked quietly. 'I can't remember when I enjoyed an evening more. I like being with you.'

She gripped his fingers, her head still bent, and spent the rest of the journey running the fingers of her other hand over the bracelet. Kurt leaned back against the seat. The vinyl was cold on his skin through the thin cotton shirt. He barely noticed the discomfort, intent on Penny's profile. Her features gave nothing away. She was so lost in thought that when their cab finally pulled up outside her house, she raised her head with a start.

Kurt asked the driver to wait whilst he accompanied her up the short walk to the front door. The night was dark; cold and still around them. When they reached the top of the path, Penny turned, sliding his jacket from her shoulders.

'Thanks for the jacket. And thank you for the bracelet. It's been a lovely evening.'

'Yes, it has. A lovely evening.'

He reached to take the jacket from her, intending to kiss her cheek as he had done once before. But then the tilt of her uplifted face, her parted lips close to his, and the nearness of her naked shoulders filled his senses, and his hand moved to touch the smooth skin of her cheek. When her face turned into his palm, he pulled her forward slowly, and then her lips were under his at last, soft and warm as he knew they would be. He moved both arms around her and held her to him, feeling her mouth open under his in thrilling invitation. She tilted her head, and his arms tightened about her. Her lips, sweet as plums, were a drug to his senses. When he finally released her, her eyes were wide open, gazing up at him, dark like the night around them. He ran a finger down her neck and to her breastbone, following the trail of it with his gaze.

'All evening . . . ' His voice drifted away as he followed the line of his finger down her cool skin. He lifted his eyes to hers. 'I've been thinking of this all evening.' His mouth found hers again, and he kissed her harder. She uttered a soft moan, and he tried to draw back, but the desire he had held in check for so long caught him in its grip. With an effort, he lifted his head. She shivered, bereft of the warmth of his arms around her, and he caught her face in his hand.

'I don't want to leave you,' he said tightly. She didn't move. Her eyes were on his, dark and serious. 'I'll see you tomorrow, OK?' he urged. 'You'll come?'

He searched her face, and when she nodded, he gave a small smile.

'See you tomorrow,' she said. Her voice was hardly a whisper. And then she reached up and kissed his mouth gently, and the flame leapt up again and raged within him. She stepped back, twisted the knob on the door to open it, and was gone.

* * *

The house was silent when Penny entered. Her grandfather had left a light on in the hallway, but the rest of the house was in darkness. He would be in his room, she thought, either sleeping or retired to bed. He would want to leave her some privacy.

One day you'll find the man who truly loves you. And sooner than you think. She remembered his words and the smile that accompanied them, and she closed her eyes. She leaned back against the front door and wrapped her arms around her burning body.

Kurt had given her roses. He overheard her say she liked the diamond bracelet, and he had gone out of his way to grant her wish. And he'd kissed her. He'd seen her home and kissed her goodnight on her doorstep. She hugged herself. For a man who declared himself an enemy of romance, he wasn't doing badly. Then a small voice of doubt spoke in her head, and her eyes flew open. She stared down the hallway, and a cold feeling seeped into the pit of her stomach. What if her dreams were running away with her? Maybe tomorrow, in the cold light of day, Kurt would come to his senses and realise Penny Rosas just wasn't the type of woman for him. Perhaps he'd think ending their evening by kissing her was a big mistake. She gripped her fingers together, assailed by terrible fear. She knew she was in love, all right. But she had no idea of Kurt's feelings. No idea at all.

She continued to stare straight ahead for several minutes. Finally, she summoned the will to pull herself upright and away from the door. Her eyes fell on the bouquet of white roses which her grandfather had placed in a vase on the hall table. Kurt had brought her roses. Not tulips or any other flower this time, but roses. Surely that had to mean something?

Before the ball, and before Kurt's kiss, Penny had resolved that tomorrow would be their final meeting. Now the perfume of the flowers filled her mind with an almost unbearable sense of hope. She moved a finger over the opening blooms, and a couple of petals drifted to the floor, as fragile as the hope that filled her.

Suddenly, and with a sick sense of anxiety, she remembered Kurt had still to see the bedroom she created for him. If he hadn't guessed at the depth of her feelings when she kissed him, he surely would when he saw the passionate transformation she had made of that room. She had thrown all of herself into that space, leaving no neutrality and no doubt as to her feelings.

And she knew then with certainty that the next day would decide everything.

* * *

Penny let herself in Kurt's front door to be met with the surprising aroma of freshly ground coffee. She made her way to the kitchen. A jug was bubbling on the range, and Kurt was hunkered down by the oven door, feeding small chunks of wood on the fire. He straightened at the sound of her footsteps, and a heart-stopping smile lit his face.

'Hey,' he said. 'Sleep well?'

He looked fresh and rested, and his eyes were filled with such warmth, all her previous anxiety melted away in a spine-tingling, flooding glow. She began to answer his question with an automatic yes and then stopped and shook her head.

'Actually, no,' she said honestly. 'I didn't sleep too well. I was thinking too much.'

He took a few steps across the room. At first glance, she had thought he looked rested, but as he neared her, Penny could see there were faint shadows under his eyes. He stood in front of her, and she caught his familiar aroma, like the skin on fresh apples.

'I've been thinking, too,' he said. He took a slow step nearer. 'And one of the things that kept me awake was thinking how much I liked kissing you. And how much I wanted to kiss you again.'

He lifted a hand to her face. This time when his lips met hers, she could sense the urgency of his kiss in the tightening of his arms around her. She pressed herself to him, giving herself up to the luxury of his hard embrace with a fierce, tight joy. For a long while, she clung to him until Kurt broke their kiss gently, lifting his head and pressing his forehead to hers.

'Come and sit for a while, and we can talk,' he said softly. 'I made you some real coffee. Real Wyoming coffee, that is. Good for people who've had sleepless nights.'

He turned to the oak table and pulled out a chair for her. 'And I bought us some bacon and eggs.' He smiled. 'A real Wyoming breakfast. See, you've made me feel at home here already.'

He went to a cupboard to get them both a couple of mugs.

'Have you looked round the rest of the house yet?' Penny asked anxiously.

'No, not yet.' He turned, mugs in hand. 'I was waiting for you.'

Penny didn't know whether to be glad or sorry. On the one hand, she wanted very much to be there to see Kurt's reaction when he walked into his bedroom. On the other, she knew the room itself would reveal everything about how she felt for him, and the thought terrified her.

When he put a steaming cup of black coffee in front of her, she took a large gulp, almost burning her mouth.

'Hey, careful.' He reached out a hand to take the mug from her and then checked himself. 'I don't want to do the big brother thing again but be careful. It's hot.'

Penny recalled how she'd snapped at him in the hotel lobby the previous night, and a faint heat stole into her cheeks. He pulled out the chair next to hers and sat down away from the table, resting his elbows on his knees. Then he reached forward to take one of her hands in his.

'I think you must know by now I don't think of you as a kid sister.' There was a warmth in his eyes and a soft lift to his mouth. 'That's definitely not how I think of you.'

Penny felt the warm pressure of his fingers. 'I guessed not,' she said. Her cheeks dimpled. 'That wasn't a very brotherly kiss last night. And when I was lying awake last night I was thinking about kissing you again, too.'

He reached forward as though to take her in his arms, but she lifted a hand and held it up between them, the smile leaving her eyes. 'But when I was awake last night I was also thinking of what you said earlier. What about your plans for the future?' She tilted her head to indicate the kitchen. 'I mean, you bought this house because you were planning to get married and everything. And you've been dating other women. I know how important it is to you to get married and start a family. I just don't see . . . ' Her sentence trailed away, but her blue eyes were back on him, alive with question.

'Yes,' he said. 'I know what you must be thinking. I've been dating, but nothing's really come of it.' He leaned back, frowning down at their joined hands. 'I don't know what it is. I had a plan for the future all mapped out, right enough, but nothing's turned out like I thought.' He raised his head as though his own words had surprised him. 'I've had lots of dates these past few months. But you're the only person I've really liked being with.'

Penny stilled, her eyes on his, waiting for him to continue. But Kurt, who was normally so direct, and spoke at all times with conviction, hesitated. The silence stretched a little too long. Penny drew her fingers slowly out of his and brought her hand to rest on the table top. She was still gazing at him intently, looking for any sign, any meaning she could recognise in his impassive features, but there was nothing.

'Do you mean you enjoy my company?' She couldn't help the slight note of chill that crept into her voice. Kurt drew back.

'Yes . . . I mean, no. No, of course it's not just that. It's . . . ' He broke off, and for the first time since Penny had met him, he appeared to be at a loss.

'What is it?' she asked quietly.

He raised his grey eyes to hers, and

she looked straight into their depths but could guess at nothing. He leaned towards her, and his hands rested on her arms with extraordinary gentleness. Everything in the way he moved, the intensity of his expression, the softness of his touch, spoke of the depth of his feelings. But his words — his words said nothing.

He carried on speaking, his gaze unwavering. 'You're not like anyone else I've ever dated. And the thought of spending more time with you . . . well, I can't tell you how happy that would make me. When I kissed you last night, I knew for certain . . . ' He took in a deep breath, his eyes steady on hers. 'I knew for certain that I didn't want anyone else but you. And I knew for certain I was going to ask you to marry me.'

Penny went totally still. Too amazed even to gasp out loud, she stared into his eyes, in the depths of which she now recognised uncertainty and hope. She drew her head back and felt his fingers tighten on her arms.

'It's good that you like spending time with me,' she said. Her voice was hollow, and she measured each word as she continued. 'But I'm not really sure enjoying each other's company is enough. I'm not sure we're the same people. You told me you were looking for someone who shared the same values. You told me passionate love was for idiots.'

The colour left Kurt's face, leaving the shadows beneath his eyes etched in dark relief. 'I still believe that,' he said fiercely. 'I believe we could have something really good between us, without all the drama. Don't force me down that path.' He gripped her arms unconsciously. 'I would do everything in my power to make you happy. Are you honestly telling me you couldn't be happy with me?'

His eyes bored into hers, willing her to answer as he wanted. She stood and pulled away from him, scraping her chair back. He stood with her, dropping his hands to his sides. She took a few steps backwards towards the kitchen units and leaned back on them. She had never imagined this. He had asked her to marry him! And could she be happy? In her sleepless dreams of the previous evening, she would have said yes. A thousand — a million times! — *yes*. But now . . . why did he refuse to say the words she so desperately needed to hear? The thought leapt to her mind, no matter how she strove against it, that he was looking for someone to marry — that he had a plan for the future — and that Penny Rosas was simply the best he could find. That he didn't really love her the way a man loved a woman but was content to marry her because they *enjoyed each other's company*. That in the end, she was second-best, like she normally was.

She refused to believe it. She lifted her head and fixed her eyes on him where he stood rigid, waiting for her answer.

'I know you don't like drama,' she

said quietly, trying desperately to keep her voice level — to keep the pleading out of her tone. 'But answer me this just once, and I won't ask you again. Do you actually love me?'

She saw a spark flash in his eyes, but he kept his voice under rigid control. 'I won't lie to you. I'm not going to say words I think are meaningless. If you're asking for romantic love, you're pinning your hopes on a dream. Why not take what we have and be happy?'

A jumble of words and feelings rushed through Penny's exhausted brain in a whirling flood. She saw a future stretch before her as Kurt's wife, living in his house, with their children even, and wondered would this be happiness? He would be good to her and would be a good father. Wouldn't any woman call that happiness?

She gazed at him without speaking, trying to control the feelings rushing chaotically through her. She had no idea what was the right course of action. She had a dream — a dream where she could share her love equally with a man who loved her in return without reservation. A dream where marriage involved all the romance of falling in love — not a logical agreement between two people who got on well. If she married Kurt, would she be selling out on her dream?

Exasperated at her silence, Kurt uttered the words that were to cause him bitter regret. He stepped forward impatiently. 'You're being ridiculously romantic.'

Penny blanched. They were the same words David had flung at her. If she needed anything to help her make her mind up, that was it.

Instantly, Kurt leapt forward, his hand outstretched towards her, but it was too late. Penny turned to pick up the jacket she'd left lying on the kitchen worktop.

'I'm sorry, Kurt,' she said. Her breath seemed to have deserted her, and her fingers were trembling, but she turned to face him squarely. 'I think we're two different people. We've had a great time together. It's been fun.' She cringed inwardly at what she was saying but forced herself to carry on. 'And it's very tempting to think we could continue this way, but in the end I don't think we'd be happy. Granddad told me not to accept second-best. If you're not in love with me, then that's what I'd be doing.'

She waited, giving him every opportunity, willing him to say the words, but he said nothing, his lips a thin, pale line. She reached into the pocket of her jacket, and an unbearable sadness swept over her.

'Here,' she said, holding out his house keys. He continued to gaze at her, ignoring the keys as though incapable of moving. She reached behind her and placed the keys on the worktop. 'I'm sorry. I can't change who I am.' Her voice trembled at her last words, and he took a few swift steps forwards, reaching out a hand, but she turned away.

'Bye, Kurt.'

She took a few swift steps to the door and then almost ran down the echoing hallway, leaving him rooted to the spot. The front door swung to with sickening finality behind her.

★ ★ ★

It was a long time before Kurt moved. The emptiness of the house without Penny's presence came crashing down around his ears, and the blood pounded through his head. He had driven her away. He would give up all he had in the world for her, but terror had frozen the words on his lips. And now the very thing he had been so afraid of losing was lost to him. He had lost Penny.

He sank down in the chair she had so recently vacated and placed his head in his hands, unconsciously adopting the same pose his father had all those years ago, when his step-mother had left them. For a long time he sat like this, the thoughts whirling uselessly around in his head, until the pounding in his temples subsided, and the quiet of the house overwhelmed him. Then he leapt up, anxious to break the hideous silence. He needed to be doing something, anything to wipe away the last image of her, those blue eyes swimming with hurt.

He strode aimlessly, seeing her hand in every tiny detail in his house. The thought came to him that she'd appeared anxious to show him his finished bedroom. He stood uncertainly at the bottom of the staircase, his hand on the banister. Memories of their first day together in the house came flooding back: the way she'd stood on the landing, gazing out at the park; the way she'd darted through the house throwing open doors and windows, letting light and air chase out the drabness and dust. All of a sudden, he needed to know how she'd finished the last room. Overwhelmed with curiosity, he took the stairs two at a time. The bedroom door was ajar. He pushed it wide and halted in the doorway, blinking slowly.

The light from the window filtered through the room, illuminating the walls. The deep azure of the sky outside and the blue of the paintwork merged as one, spreading a soft, cerulean hue around him. It was the colour of Penny's eyes, and in Kurt's state of heightened sensibility, it was as though he had stepped physically inside her gentle body, and the glow of her touch was all around him. For a few minutes he stood there, bathed in light, his heart slowing its race as the wondrous hue washed over him.

He stepped carefully into the centre of the room, anxious not to break the astonishing spell the light cast over him.

A large wooden bedstead, painted white, framed the king-size mattress. On either side were white wooden tables, on one of which Penny had placed a simple vase of purple irises. Kurt stilled. So overwhelmed was he by the events of the morning and the gentle beauty of the room that for a long while he remained motionless. Gradually he raised his head to note with wonder a series of richly coloured paintings along one wall. He turned slowly.

In the first canvas, a man and a woman lay under an astonishing patchwork of flowers. The blossoms formed a sensuous quilt of blues, violets, and gold. The couple's naked arms were entwined above the coverlet, their eyes closed as if in sleep. The woman's head was tilted, the bow of her rosy mouth lifting at the corners, and her features bathed in bliss. Kurt stared at her for what seemed an age, his senses drugged with the dreamlike beauty of the reclining figures.

In the next painting, the same couple. This time, they embraced under the man's golden cloak beneath the branches of a leafless tree. Only the woman's face was visible, tilted back in the man's arms, the same expression of bliss on her parted lips and in her eyes, visible beneath the barely open eyelids.

The branches of the tree reached for the heavens in a passionate swirl of gold.

It was the painting over the bed that caused Kurt to linger longest. The couple were kneeling, so entirely swathed in their cloak of patterned gold that only their heads and the woman's naked feet appeared out of the rich colour. The man had caught the woman's face in his hands and was bending to kiss her, her arm flung around his neck to pull him close. The woman's pale face was tilted to receive his kiss, and she was leaning into him with such an expression of passionate, exquisite abandon that Kurt was overcome with an emotion so intense it robbed him of the power to breathe.

After several minutes, he laid himself down on the bed, arms spread wide on either side of him, allowing the intense passion of the room to wash over him. In all his life, he had never felt such an intensity of emotion. He thought of Penny and was filled with a mixture of joy — joy at what she had created for him — and crushing grief that she was lost to him.

He closed his eyes, and the blue light from the window streamed over his rigid figure, shining through his closed lids. The couple above the bed clung to their embrace.

★   ★   ★

The first thing Penny saw when she returned from Kurt's house was the wilting bouquet of white roses. The hallway was filled with the perfume of decay. She glared at the innocent blooms as she passed them on the way to her room.

'You'll be dead soon anyway, stupid flowers,' she cried. 'And what was the point of you, anyway?'

Immediately, she felt ashamed of herself and turned back foolishly. 'I'm sorry. It's not your fault.' The inanimate roses bent their heads. 'It's not even Kurt's fault. It's my fault for imagining someone like me could ever be loved the way I want. The way I love him.'

Her voice broke, and she knew she was dangerously close to tears. It was silly and useless, but she had the house to herself, and so she was able to sit down on the stairs, put her head in her hands, and indulge in a fit of crying which, although it did nothing to ease the pain, gave her some relief from the thoughts whirling uselessly round her head.

'I don't even know why he gave me roses, anyway,' she confided in the flowers through her sobs. 'What sort of flowers are they to bring? Doesn't he know anything?'

She turned and took the stairs to her room, still sobbing. The sight of her evening dress and silk wrap hanging from the wardrobe door caused her misery to intensify, and she threw herself face down on the bed and cried as though her heart were literally breaking inside her chest.

For days she had steeled herself for

the final meeting with Kurt, and she had been preparing to say goodbye and walk away. All her trusty barriers had been in place, and as far as possible she had been mentally resolved. But then he had kissed her, and everything changed. She had felt what it was to be in his arms, and she had kissed him back with all the passion of her being.

She sat up on the bed with a start. His bedroom! By now, he would have seen the paintings. She gave a groan and threw herself back down on the bed, burying her face in the pillow. If the way she'd kissed him last night hadn't already told him, the paintings in his bedroom definitely would. He would know for certain how passionately, deeply in love she was with him.

She screwed the pillow around her face. She was in love with him — and he had told her he *enjoyed her company*. She wouldn't accept him on those terms. Never! She dropped her pillow, dried her eyes, and swung her legs off the bed.

She had always known deep down that those dreams of happiness weren't for her. She wasn't the woman her mother had been, and she never would be. Her romantic dreams were never going to come true, but that didn't mean she couldn't take control of her life. She would just have to turn her life in another direction, that's all.

She stood up and lifted the evening dress from its hook. She would have it cleaned and returned to its place in the trunk. Cinderella's ball was over, and in real life, there was never going to be a handsome prince to come looking for her. And there were never going to be any stupid happy ever afters, either, she thought. It was all just getting on with your life day after day.

In total thrall to her unhappiness, she threw herself back on the bed and wept anew.

11

' . . . and so the figures are confirmed in this final graph here.' Alex flicked onto the next slide of his presentation. 'Thought you might like a hard copy for the next board report?'

Kurt gazed abstractedly at the laptop in front of them, only half listening.

'I said I thought you might like a hard copy if those figures are useful?' Alex repeated, looking straight at him. Still no response. 'I said, Kurt, you're the biggest idiot this side of the Atlantic.'

'What?' Kurt turned with blank eyes and then nodded his head. 'Yeah, that sounds great. Thanks.'

Alex leaned across to grip Kurt's shoulder, applying a gentle pressure. 'Hey,' he said. 'Are you doing OK? You look like crap. Have you seen yourself lately?'

Kurt didn't need Alex to point out anything about his appearance. He'd seen the black shadows under his eyes every day in the mirror for the past six weeks. He shrugged off his friend's hand.

'Yeah, guess I haven't been sleeping so good lately. Maybe the city doesn't agree with me.' He lifted his head to the view of gleaming tower blocks outside his office window. 'I've been thinking of heading back to Wyoming.'

Alex stared at him for a few minutes without speaking. Then he dropped his hand from Kurt's shoulder. 'What would you do a damn fool thing like that for?' he asked quietly. 'Seems to me you'd be running away.'

Kurt lifted his head.

'Seems to me that would be a coward's way out,' Alex continued. 'You might be an idiot, but I never had you pegged as a coward.'

A spark finally lit in Kurt's deadened heart. 'I'm no coward,' he said fiercely. 'But I'd sooner face a raging bull alone in a pen than . . . than end up half-crazed again like this.'

Alex shook his head and sank back in his chair. 'Kurt, you're already half-crazed,' he said eventually. He gave a short laugh. 'God knows, I'm not the person to give advice. But I tell you something — I've never in my life seen anyone as miserable as you these past few weeks. Go and get the girl.' He stood and picked up his laptop, then leaned over the table and said quietly, 'Take a risk on her before someone else does. Because I'm telling you, you're a fool if you lose her.'

★ ★ ★

The bell over the shop door jangled its familiar chime as Kurt pushed it open. The very first time he'd stepped into Penny's shop a cold drizzle had been trickling down from a grey sky. Today the sun was out in force, and the streets were dry and dusty. The weather wasn't the only change. Kurt scanned his eyes around the shop to find Tehmeena sitting behind Penny's desk. A young man in short sleeves stood behind the counter. There was no sign of Penny.

Tehmeena jumped up at the sight of him and stepped forward in surprise. 'Hello.'

She stretched on her toes and greeted him with a polite kiss on the cheek, her brown eyes full of a rather frosty enquiry. 'What brings you here? Do you need something for your house?'

Kurt cleared his throat. 'No, actually I'd just come to see Penny. Is she here?'

He felt rather uncomfortable under Tehmeena's cool scrutiny. Her usual banter appeared to have vanished, and she was looking at him in an appraising way that made him feel even more ill at ease than ever, if that were possible.

'Actually, Penny isn't here,' she said eventually. Her eyebrows lifted. 'Didn't you know?'

'No.' His heart plummeted sickeningly. 'No, she didn't say. Where did she go?'

Tehmeena continued to search his face for a minute or two. Then the shop door jangled again, letting in another customer. She swivelled her head before turning back to look at him.

'You really didn't know?'

Kurt shook his head, a cold fear rising from the pit of his stomach. Tehmeena regarded him thoughtfully whilst he stood there waiting, taut with anxiety. 'Fine,' she said eventually. 'I'll meet you in the pub over the road at twelve. OK?'

Twelve? That was hours away. It was all Kurt could do not to grip Tehmeena's arms and beg her to tell him where Penny had gone. Something in his expression must have shown, because she began to usher him to the door.

'Twelve o'clock,' she said firmly. 'High Noon, cowboy. Wait 'til then.'

Kurt resisted the temptation to plant himself outside the door, waiting with his face pressed agonisingly to the glass. For a couple of hours he wandered the streets aimlessly, the sick feeling growing with every second. Finally, he came upon the banks of the Thames and sat down on a stone bench to rest his head on his fists.

What an idiot he was. He'd been terrified of trusting Penny, of revealing the depths of his love for her, because he was frightened of losing his mind to passion. And now this. The worst of it was remembering the hurt in her eyes when she'd left his house. Time and time again her expression and the exact way her head bent, replayed in his mind, like a videotape stuck on loop. And now she was gone, and it was all too late. Maybe Alex was right. Maybe she'd already found someone else. And it would serve him right if she had, because quite honestly, he didn't deserve her.

The brown, sluggish waters inched by interminably until it was time to stand up and retrace his steps. When he finally pushed open the heavy swing doors of the Edwardian pub he couldn't help but remember the last time he'd been there, waiting for Penny at a table by the window, and how his heart lifted at the sight of her, even then, when he hardly knew her. How long ago it all seemed now.

He ordered himself a bourbon and sat down at that same table in the window. When Tehmeena finally pushed open the door of the pub, the anxiety coursing through him surged and peaked. He stood hastily and pulled out a chair for her, watching her sink into it. Then she raised her frank brown gaze to his.

'I've only got a few minutes,' she said. 'I've had to leave our new guy in charge, and he's only been with us a few weeks.'

'Thanks for coming. I can't tell you how much it means. She never told me . . . I mean, can you tell me where she's gone?' He tried to keep the desperation from his voice, but he could tell from the sympathetic way Tehmeena was beginning to look at him that he was probably failing.

'She's gone to Italy.'

'What?' Kurt pulled back, astounded. 'Why Italy? I mean — ' A sudden terrible thought occurred to him. 'Has she gone alone?'

'Yes, yes,' Tehmeena said, waving an impatient hand. 'Of course she's alone. She hasn't met anyone else, if that's what you mean. She's been mooning over you for long enough. She's taken six months off work to go travelling. Said it's something she always wanted to do, so she's combining her trip with searching for new sources of antiques for the shop. We've taken on a new guy, and I've taken David's place as joint partner.'

'Yeah?' Kurt looked up abstractedly. 'Congratulations on that.'

'Thanks,' Tehmeena said drily. There was a couple of minutes silence whilst Kurt stared fixedly at his empty bourbon glass. 'Well,' she continued, starting to get up, 'I'm running short of time . . .'

'No, don't go.' He reached a hand out, and Tehmeena dropped back into her seat, a patient and interested expression on her face.

'Where's she gone?' he said hurriedly. 'I mean, where exactly in Italy? And for how long?'

'She's in Florence at the moment. She's there for another week, and then she's moving on to Rome.'

'OK, I need your help,' he said. 'And I need to go back into the shop. There's something I need to buy.'

He bent his head over the table, and Tehmeena bent forward to listen, agog.

★　★　★

A small bead of perspiration trickled down Penny's back. The stone stairs that led up to the Piazzale Michelangelo were never-ending, and the early evening air was hot and dusty.

Why on earth am I doing this? she asked herself, allowing a giggling group of teenagers to overtake her. She'd had an odd call from Tehmeena that morning, asking her to take a photo of the sunset over Florence. And it had to be taken from the top of the longest climb in probably all of Italy. It would be romantic, Tehmeena had promised her, and wasn't she looking for romance? Penny just snorted.

She'd just spent a week in Venice — the most romantic city in Europe — photographing everything she saw, only to realise that for her, romance must be dead. She'd stood in St Mark's Square and felt nothing. She doubted Michelangelo's square was going to make her feel any better.

There was a small crowd milling in the enormous, dusty Piazza when she finally reached the top. She pulled out her camera and made her way to the stone balustrade on the western side to where the sun was making its descent.

'Actually, this was worth the climb,' she admitted grudgingly. To the west flowed the River Arno, with its three ancient stone bridges arching gracefully across, and a little beyond was the magnificent red dome of the Duomo Cathedral. A row of tall ochre and red stone buildings lined the river. Penny put her elbows on the wall and leaned out. A faint breeze stirred the warm air. The sun was sinking lower over the horizon, the gathering dusk creeping in softly behind it. The reflections of the city lights were beginning to ripple in the waters of the river.

A footstep behind her caused her to stiffen. She hoped she wouldn't have to fend off any male attention. Since she'd arrived in Italy, she'd noted with irony that just when she'd decided to devote her life to being a spinster and a mad cat lady, men seemed to pop up from all over the place intent on getting to know her. She was forever fending off advances.

She turned a cold shoulder and leaned further over the wall.

The steps came nearer, and she caught a familiar scent. Like the skin on fresh apples. Her breath caught in her throat.

'Penny.'

She whirled round at the sound of his voice, dropping her camera to the ground. The leather case hit the stones with an expensive thud. It was no dream. He was standing there in front of her, a little leaner, the shadows a little deeper under his eyes. She stared, not speaking.

He took another step forward. 'Tehmeena told me where you were. I had to see you before it was too late. I wanted to tell you . . . ' He took a breath.

In the mad whirl of her thoughts, Penny noted he had a slim, rectangular box in one hand, and that the fingers holding it were clenched tight. His eyes were steady on hers.

'I wanted to tell you before it was too late that I love you. And when I saw the room you made for me, I thought . . . that gave me hope that I might not have ruined everything. I love you beyond distraction. I love you, Penny Rosas, and the thought I may have lost you has me half-crazed.' His words came in a trembling rush, so unlike his usual measured tones. His eyes stayed fixed on hers. She didn't speak. He took another step forward.

'I brought you this,' he said, holding the box out slowly. 'But if you tell me you don't want it . . . '

He was near enough now for Penny to make out the pulse beating quickly under the warm skin of his throat. He extended his hand, and she reached out her own to take the box from him wordlessly.

'If you tell me you don't want it, I'll leave. But after that, I don't know what the hell I'll do.'

There was a whiteness to his lips and in the faint lines around his nostrils.

Penny lifted the lid of the box. Some crumpled tissue paper and then the dying rays of the sun caught a cluster of tiny rose diamonds. She lifted the jewels in a hand that was suddenly shaking.

Two shimmering pearls caught in a silver heart. The love token.

She raised her eyes to Kurt's, brimming with tears of wonder. 'How . . . ?' she asked. The words caught in her throat. She held the box away from her as though it were unreal.

'I wanted you to have your dream.' He turned his head to take in the sunset and the lights of the city below them. 'I begged Tehmeena to get you to come here. I wanted to ask you to marry me, and I wanted it to be perfect.' His gaze roved her face and fastened on her wide eyes. 'I wanted it to be romantic for you. I was scared I'd left it too late.'

Her eyes dropped to the love token in her hands. The silver chain played out through her fingers.

'I want you to know how much I love you,' he said again, taking a step forward.

Her head lifted quickly, her eyes brimming with unimaginable joy, and she almost leapt forward into his arms.

His hands fastened around her, and his mouth was on hers, gently at first. Then his arms tightened, his hungry mouth devoured her, and she gasped with the most delicious burst of golden euphoria lifting and swirling her body.

A passing group whistled. He drew back, looking down at her.

'What an idiot I've been,' he said, a tremor in his voice. 'I was frightened of losing you. So frightened of ending up half-crazed, I was out of my senses. I'm sorry I hurt you.'

She reached a hand up to his lips. 'Is this a dream?' she asked softly. He shook his head. The well of happiness within filled to overflowing.

'Then dreams can come true, after all,' she whispered. She reached up and met his lips with her own, closing her fingers around the love token and wrapping her arms around his neck in a long, long embrace, whilst the sun set behind them over the Arno.

We do hope that you have enjoyed reading this large print book.

Did you know that all of our titles are available for purchase?

We publish a wide range of high quality large print books including:
Romances, Mysteries, Classics
General Fiction
Non Fiction and Westerns

Special interest titles available in large print are:
The Little Oxford Dictionary
Music Book, Song Book
Hymn Book, Service Book

Also available from us courtesy of Oxford University Press:
Young Readers' Dictionary
(large print edition)
Young Readers' Thesaurus
(large print edition)

For further information or a free brochure, please contact us at:
Ulverscroft Large Print Books Ltd.,
The Green, Bradgate Road, Anstey,
Leicester, LE7 7FU, England.
Tel: (00 44) **0116 236 4325**
Fax: (00 44) **0116 234 0205**

THE FERRYBOAT

Kate Blackadder

When Judy and Tom Jeffrey are asked by their daughter Holly and her Scottish chef husband Corin if they will join them in buying the Ferryboat Hotel in the West Highlands, they take the plunge and move north. The rundown hotel needs much expensive upgrading, and what with local opposition to some of their plans — and worrying about their younger daughter, left down south with her flighty grandma — Judy begins to wonder if they've made a terrible mistake . . .

MEET ME AT MIDNIGHT

Gael Morrison

Nate Robbins needs the money bequeathed to him by his eccentric uncle — but in order to get it he must remarry before his thirtieth birthday, three weeks away. Deserted by her husband, Samantha Feldon is determined not to marry again unless she's sure the love she finds is true. So when her boss — Nate Robbins — offers her the job of 'wife', she refuses, but agrees to help him find someone suitable. Accompanying him on a Caribbean cruise, Sam finds him the perfect woman — realizing too late she loves Nate herself . . .

LOOKING FOR LAURIE

Beth James

On finding a dead body in her flat, Laurie Kendal fights her instinct to scream, and instead races to the nearest police station. About to embark upon a cycling holiday, DI Tom Jessop attends the scene, only to find . . . nothing! The body has inexplicably disappeared, and so he dismisses Laurie's story as rubbish. But there is something intriguing about Laurie — she is beautifully eccentric, yet vulnerable too, and earnest in her insistence that her story is true. So before starting his holiday, Tom has one more check on her flat . . .

A CHRISTMAS ENGAGEMENT

Jill Barry

Adjusting to life without her late husband, Molly Reid is determined to make the most of a holiday to Madeira. As the dreamlike days of surf and sun pass, a friendship with her tour guide Michael develops and grows, though she wonders whether his attention and care are just part of his job. Back in Wales, meanwhile, Molly's daughter and son-in-law are hatching a surprise family reunion over Christmas — and it looks like the family could be about to gain some new members . . .

LOVE ON HOLD

Dorothy Taylor

Following a broken engagement, Rosa takes up a friend's offer to work on her Anglesey holiday cottage. When she meets her new neighbour, brooding Welsh farmer Gareth, a powerful mutual attraction flares between them, and she agrees to work on his upcoming barn conversion. But the rich, stylish Erin seems to have staked a claim on Gareth — and Rosa's ex-fiancé Nick is harassing her. Can Rosa and Gareth forge a relationship together — or will their pasts catch up with them and ruin everything?